PORCUPINE

● ● ● ● ● ● ● ● ● ● ● ● ● ●

MEG TILLY

TUNDRA BOOKS

Published in Canada by Tundra Books,
75 Sherbourne Street, Toronto, Ontario M5A 2P9

Published in the United States by Tundra Books of Northern New York,
P.O. Box 1030, Plattsburgh, New York 12901

Library of Congress Control Number: 2007923878

Library and Archives Canada Cataloguing in Publication

Tilly, Meg
Porcupine / Meg Tilly.

ISBN 978-0-88776-810-1

I. Title.

PS8589.I54P67 2007   jC813'.54   C2006-906924-7

We acknowledge the financial support of the Government of Canada through the Book
Publishing Industry Development Program (BPIDP) and that of the Government of Ontario
through the Ontario Media Development Corporation's Ontario Book Initiative.
We further acknowledge the support of the Canada Council for the Arts and the Ontario Arts
Council for our publishing program.

ONTARIO ARTS COUNCIL
CONSEIL DES ARTS DE L'ONTARIO

Design: Terri Nimmo
Printed in Canada

1 2 3 4 5 6   12 11 10 09 08 07

To my little sister, Becky,
who taught me porcupines could be petted

● ● ● ● ● ● ● ● ● ● ● ● ● ● ● ● ●

PORCUPINE

● ● ● ● ● ● ● ● ● ● ● ● ● ● ●

AUTUMN

I'm sitting in my favorite spot when I hear Mom's footsteps. If I hadn't been so excited that the morning fog had finally lifted, letting me see clear out past the harbor to Cape Spear, I would have heard her sooner and jumped down quick. But it's too late for that now.

I hold still and hope she doesn't look my way. I hear her walk past my bedroom. She must be going down the hall to my kid sister Tessa's room. Yes! I'm home free, but then Mom stops, backtracks. I should have shut the door. It's really too late now. She's standing in my doorway. I can feel her glaring at me, hands on her hips. I don't see her with my eyes, as my back is to the room. I have my window open wide and am sitting with my butt all comfy on the ledge, my legs and feet sticking outside. It looks scarier than it is. It's really no big deal, my feet are keeping me perfectly balanced on the black asphalt-tile roof. Little steel-blue and silver flecks sprinkled throughout glint in the morning sun.

"*Jacqueline!* What in God's name do you think you're doing?"

"Looking at Cape Spear," I say. "It's a nice clear day." I'm not trying to be a smart-ass, just stating the facts. This is the best spot in the house. Hell, it's probably the best view in the whole wide world. You can see forever, out over the tops of the houses, to the ocean and beyond. Every once in a while if I'm lucky, I get to see a faraway iceberg floating past. I love that. I feel like I'm sending voyagers off on their journey. Where will the icebergs go? Where will they end up? How long can they travel before they're all melted and gone? They're really beautiful to see, kind of mysterious. When one of the sun's rays comes out through the clouds and hits one of these babies, it's so beautiful your breath stops in your throat and you think you're going to die. People travel from all over to see these icebergs, and I get to hop up on my windowsill and see them for free. I love it here. It makes me feel peaceful, the brisk salt air on my face, with just a kiss of the ocean. Sometimes I can taste a hint of it on my lips when I climb back inside. Don't get it in the same way down on the street. See, there's something about looking out on the world like this, from this high-up vantage point, makes me feel like the world's going to be okay. Watching the ships coming and going, playing guessing games as to where they're from, where they're going next. Who needs TV when I have this view any time I want.

But Mom? She just doesn't understand. I've tried to get her out on the ledge. I've tried to show her how safe it is, how it would be almost impossible for me to slip and fall, tumble to my death. "Give me some credit," I've told her. "I'm twelve years old, Mom. It's not like I'm a baby." I've tried explaining to her: "Yes, the roof is steep, but it's rough, like a cat's tongue, and it gives me really good grip. See how I grip with my toes? I can't fall, Mom!"

She doesn't care. My mom is not the most practical woman in the world. Logic doesn't work very well on her. And I'm not trying to be harsh, but in describing my mom, the word *airhead* might come to mind. Not in a disrespectful way. Just telling the truth.

"Get down from there right now!" she says. She's using her deep voice, so I know she means business. I get down quick.

"Sorry," I say, even though I'm not. I move fast, slip past her. I am out in the hall and halfway down the stairs before she sucks enough oxygen into her lungs to launch into her lecture.

"Jacqueline! I don't want to catch you hanging out that window again! You hear me?"

"Uh-huh, yep, I hear you," I say. How could I not? She's bellowing so loud it's hurting my teeth. I turn round the corner to the living room, where Dad is sitting on the sofa. My little brother, Simon, is kneeling on the floor by the coffee table, hard at work. He's assembling this ridiculously complicated Lego contraption. No blueprints. He doesn't work that way. He can make these amazing constructions right out of his head. Nothing even close to what other kids do. Simon adds all kinds of things: rubber bands, batteries, skinny red and blue wires from Dad's workshop. He even takes the wheels from old Tonka trucks. Looks like this design has a medieval theme. This is Lego we're talking about. Lego! But Simon doesn't follow the rules. He's got himself a piece of wood and has made it into a battering ram. He's working on a catapult now, doesn't have it quite right, but he will, believe me, he will. Kid's only seven, but when he sets his mind to something, it gets done.

"You really going to stop sitting out there?" Dad says with a grin.

I smile back at him. "No way," I say, all jaunty. "What makes you think that?" I flop down on the sofa.

"Didn't you just say so to your mom?"

"No. I said, 'Uh-huh, yep, I hear you.' I couldn't help but hear her. She was screaming her head off." Dad starts laughing. "I agreed that I heard her. I said nothing about not sitting out of my window anymore."

"Oh, Jack." He reaches over, musses up my hair like I'm one of the guys. If someone else did that, I'd get pissed. "Don't touch the hair," I'd growl like a gangster in a movie. Not that I care so much about my hair, to be honest. But it's the principle of the thing. But my dad? He can muss my hair any time he wants. It makes me feel good. Like he loves me just the way I am, scrappy brown hair and all. Doesn't need me to be so neat and fancy like Mom and Tessa. Simon and I, we take after Dad's side of the family and I'm glad. "We should get you to law school!" Dad says, still laughing. "You'd make a damned fine lawyer." And even though I feel proud that my dad thinks I'm smart, I don't let on, that wouldn't be cool. Just keep my head forward, like I'm watching the morning *Hockey Highlights* show, and try not to smile too big. Dad settles back into the sofa, nice and comfy, takes a slurp of steaming coffee from his Tim Hortons mug. My dad is crazy about Tim Hortons coffee. He says it's the best in the world. And when I get old enough to drink coffee, Tim Hortons is going to be my choice too.

We watch the rest of *Hockey Highlights*. Mom comes down, Tessa in tow, and it's easy to see what they were doing upstairs. Mom's done something fancy with Tessa's hair. She's got it up in one of those French-braid hairdos and has woven a powder-blue-and-pink ribbon through her pale blond hair. It looks pretty in a girly-girl sort of way, but I'd never say it. Tessa's ego is big enough as it is. It's my job to keep her in line. She already looks like a fairy-tale princess, no point in letting her act like one too.

"Ew . . ." I say, because Tessa is swanning around. "Don't you think that's a little too fancy for hanging around the house?"

"I'm going into town," Tessa says with a smug smile. "Mom's taking me with her to the beauty parlor when she goes for her touch-ups. Highlights," she says, like I don't know what that means.

"I know what highlights are."

"No you don't."

"Yes I do, stupid! I wasn't born yesterday, you know." I hate it when she does that. Acts all superior, like she's the oldest instead of me. Ten years old and she thinks she's all that. Prancing around, nose in the air just because she's Mom's favorite. Two peas in a pod. Both of them blond-haired, blue-eyed, and dumb.

"You're just jealous because I get to go to town."

"I *don't* care," I snort through my nose. She's so juvenile sometimes.

"And Mom's going to buy *me* new shoes. Party shoes and maybe even a new dress to match." Smirk . . . smirk . . . Like she's so special. Sometimes I just want to haul off and smack her perfect, little porcelain-doll face. It's like nothing bad ever happens to her, she just bats her eyes and everybody loves her. They don't stop to ask themselves why.

"So?" I say.

"Fran?" Dad calls, turning down the volume on the TV. "What's this about you getting Tessa new shoes and a dress? You just got her a new pair of shoes two weeks ago. What's she need another pair for?"

"Those were running shoes," Mom says from the kitchen, just her head sticking around the doorway. "She's outgrown her party shoes and Brenda's party is tomorrow."

"I wear my runners to parties," I say. "What's the big deal?"

Tessa gives me a kick. "Stay out of it!" she hisses through her teeth. But I don't. I yell "Ouch!" really loud, leap off the sofa, and start hopping around the living room on one leg like I'm in agony. "Tessa *kicked* me! Jesus Christ, Tessa, whad'ya do that for?"

"Watch your language," Mom snaps and disappears back to the kitchen sink to bang pots and pans around in the dishwater, thinking that will end the conversation. But Dad switches off the TV and goes into the kitchen, Tessa trailing behind.

I stop yelling and hopping for two reasons. One, no one's paying attention anyway, and two, because I want to hear what they're saying. Which certainly won't happen if I'm yelling my head off.

"You spoil her, Fran," Dad says. I couldn't agree more. "She has twice what the other kids have."

"She does not," Mom says, back tense, ears red.

"Yes, she does. It's not right." He's talking low, but I can hear him. "Jack doesn't have party shoes."

"She doesn't *want* them –"

"Have you asked?" he says, cutting her off. "And what about Simon? That boy needs new shoes. His old ones are practically worn right through. You waste our money on frivo-lous things and don't pay attention to the practical."

"I don't want new shoes!" Simon bellows from the living room. "I like the ones I have. I just got them broken in."

"You need new shoes, Simon," I say. "Dad's right, they're in rough shape."

"All right!" Mom says. "I'll take Simon, but it's *not* going to be fun for him, sitting around the beauty parlor –"

"I don't wanna go!" Simon bellows.

"You're going, Simon," Dad says.

"Stupid!" Tessa hisses at Simon from the kitchen doorway. "You just gotta ruin my fun, spoil my mother-daughter day!" She stomps through the living room. "God! I hate you!" She slams the front door hard and runs out to the car, like she's a soap-opera queen. I can almost hear the violins playing. She throws herself inside the car, slams that door too.

"I don't want to go," says Simon, looking miserable now. Bad enough getting new shoes, even worse having Tessa mad at him.

"Go on, son," Dad says, coming back into the living room, trying to pretend that he and Mom didn't just have an argu-ment. "Go get your shoes on. Your mom's going to take you into town for some new running shoes. Won't that be nice?"

"I don't –" Simon starts, but I cut him off.

"Just do it," I say, and so he does. He puts on his beat-up

shoes while Mom gets her purse and car keys, and then they're out the door and gone. And I have to say, it's nice. Like a whirlwind has vacated the premises. It's peaceful. The way life ought to be.

"How about," says Dad, "we get a start on that swing?"

"Cool," I say, real casual, but I'm excited. We've been planning this project for some time now, and how perfect to do it today, with everybody out of our hair.

We get our supplies together, take them outside. I've got the thick brown rope from the basement. I carry it, looped up, over my shoulder like a rodeo cowboy and have to tilt my neck slightly to the side because there's so much rope. It's scratchy. Not that I'd tilt my head just for that. I'm not a sissy like Tessa. I can take a little itchiness. It's heavier than I thought, though. Got my right hand up to keep the loops from slipping off, but I do it in a no-big-deal way, so Dad'll think I can handle it. We're making a swing. No sweat. Don't worry about me, I've got your back, Dad. I'm not going to mess up.

Dad's rolling the tire from where we had been storing it, leaned up against the side of the house, and he's carrying his trusty Leatherman all-in-one multipurpose tool in his teeth. Good thing Mom's not here or he'd be getting a lecture on how putting metal objects like that in his mouth is why his teeth are so chipped. And, yes, Dad does have a chip or two missing from his front teeth. Not big-time, just enough to give his smile personality. Besides, Mom's logic doesn't make sense, because silverware is metal. Forks, spoons, knives – we're always putting them in and out of our mouths. How does she know it's not just regular living, eating, and drinking that's giving Dad such a crooked smile.

All that being said, I've got my Leatherman Super Tool 200 stuffed in the front pocket of my jeans. Not because of Mom's dire warnings, but because I find it handier to carry it that way.

"All right, Jack," Dad says, smiling his crinkle-faced smile at me. "Let the swing-making commence!"

● ● ● ●

It's time for Dad to go. Came so fast. It's funny. We knew it was going to happen. I mean, we've had a couple weeks to prepare. Seemed like so much time to get the heart ready. But, all of a sudden it's time for him to leave. No more putting it off. Big Mike's car has just pulled into the driveway.

"I've got to go," Dad says, getting to his feet, glancing at his watch.

"Bob," Mom says. She doesn't move, just sits still on the sofa like a statue, her hands limp in her lap. But my dad, he's a man of action. "Come on, Fran, up you get," and so she does. We all do.

Dad grabs his duffel bag leaning against the door and then out we traipse to the front porch. Dad's acting all lighthearted, has a big no-problem-here smile on his face. Hugs and kisses all around. Mom's first. Long and sweet. Full of I love you's. When he lets go and pushes back her hair, I can see Mom's trying not to cry.

"Don't worry," Dad says, but there's a sadness in his face too, just for a second. Then he turns to us kids and it's gone. He scoops Tessa up like she's lighter than a feather, that's how strong he is. Gives her a kiss and a hug. Calls her Princess, his pet name for her. "Be a comfort to your mother," he says.

"I will," Tessa promises, with this really sappy look on her face, like nothing but honey ever comes out of her mouth, when we all know that's just not true.

"Good girl," he says, putting her down.

It's Simon's turn now. Dad pretends to throw a few punches at him. A one-two combination, like that, a little fancy foot-work. Simon smiles shyly at him, doesn't pretend to box back, though. Don't know why he's so bashful around Dad. Dad wouldn't hurt a flea. "Take care, son," he says, kneeling down, ruffling Simon's hair, pulling him in for a one-armed hug, squashing Simon's face against his chest.

It's my turn now, and I think my heart is going to break, but I've got a no-problem-here smile on my face too. Just like Dad. And while Dad's looking at me, his expression gets serious. I see deep into him, and tears come even though I'm smiling. He holds me tight against his chest, I can feel his lips in my hair. My dad kissing me good-bye. I hear his voice, gruff, breaking slightly.

"Ah, Jack," he says. "What am I going to do with you?" I feel his scratchy cheek scrape mine. Feel his warm breath, his soft, rumbly voice in my ear. "Take care of your mom. Look after your brother and sister while I'm away. Will you do that for me?"

And I say, "Yes, Dad . . . yes. I will." Rubbing the tears from my eyes with my fist, scrunched tight up against Dad's chest. I feel him slip something into my hand, and I wrap my fingers around it tight. It's the warm metal and leather of his watch. "Keep it safe for me," he whispers in my ear. "I don't want it to get all beat up, running around in the bush out there." And I don't know why he's giving me his watch. He's been away many times but has never done this before. I start crying even harder because it's like he's saying good-bye for good. "Chin up," Dad says. "That's my girl," and so I straighten myself up, put a smile on my face, pull away like nothing happened, like I don't have his watch still warm from his wrist clutched in my fist.

"Okay, guys," Dad says, all jokey and boisterous, like he's a comedian on TV. "I'm off. Don't forget to write." And I wish Big Mike would drive around the block a few times, go get himself a coffee, come back later, but he doesn't. He's just sitting in his car, waiting for Dad, engine running. Dad gives

Mom another quick kiss and hug. The one-armed kind like he gave Simon, his other arm scooping up his bag.

"See you soon! Love you all!" Dad says, head turned toward us as he runs down the steps, his duffel bag bouncing slightly, banging against his back.

At first we all stand on the porch like we always do, waving good-bye. But then as the car pulls out of the driveway, something breaks and I find myself running down the steps, the walkway, out into the street after the car. Not down the street for a long way, just a few yards. And I'm waving, yelling at the top of my lungs, "Good-bye! Love you, Dad! Good-bye! Safe journey! Love you!" And so then Simon does it too. Comes out on the street with me, the two of us waving, dancing a silly good-bye dance, like we are on a string. All elbows and knees and flat, waving palms. "Bye, Dad! Love you! Bye, Dad!" And we've got big smiles on our faces, and Dad is smiling too. Can see his face turned around in the front seat of the car. I'm smiling, but there's a tightness in my chest, because Dad's going to Afghanistan, and I've seen what happens there. Seen the scary news on TV.

But when I told Dad my fears, he just laughed at me and said, "Don't worry. It's fine there now. We're a peacekeeping unit, we're not going to war. This is the Canadian Armed Forces we're taking about, not the U.S. Army. We're just going to Afghanistan to keep the peace, that's all. I'm not going to Iraq, honey. So there's no problem. Chin up, Jack, chin up. Don't look so sad. Give me a smile. That's my girl."

We wave until the car turns the corner and disappears. Then Simon and I go back up to the porch where Mom is standing with her arm around Tessa. I slip Simon under Mom's other arm and we go inside, arm in arm. We have to go in sideways so we can all fit through the door. Mom doesn't cook tonight. We go to A&W for a special treat. And we toast Dad with frosty, ice-cold, foaming mugs of root beer, and we send him our love and say a prayer for his speedy and safe return home.

● ● ● ●

Ms. Harris is standing at the front of the class in her usual spot by the side of her desk, flustered as always. She's reading out loud from the exact same sheet of paper she just handed us copies of. It's a little hard to hear her because all of the girls are still oohing and aahing over Sara's new shirt that her Aunt Linda brought back for her from New York. Which would be fine if they were sitting in another part of the room, but Sara plopped her butt right down in the seat next to me, and now she's sneak-eating some kind of fancy chocolate out from under her desk, which is causing a whispered "Can I have some?" uproar.

Obviously Ms. Harris hasn't been teaching that long; otherwise she would have quieted them down. Not only that, she'd have known that she didn't have to go from desk to desk to hand out each sheet of paper. She would've slapped a bunch of them down on the first desk in each row and said, "Take one and pass them back."

I wonder if this is her first job. She looks young enough, and she was pretty shaky the first week or so. Hands nervous, startled movements, face flushed.

"Carla saved her money and bought a mountain bike," reads Ms. Harris.

I think it's so funny how whoever writes these problem-solving questions tries to relate: "Hmm, what do kids nowadays like? I know! Mountain bikes! I'll throw a mountain bike in there and that'll make them sit up and take note!"

"Her dad had given her one hundred and seventy-nine dollars and forty-nine cents, which was half the cost of the bike." The concentration lines appear between Ms. Harris's eyebrows. I have a suspicion that these problem questions are not her strong suit. As a matter of fact, the math portion of our day always seems to make her sweat. And when someone asks her a question, she always has to refer to the book before she answers. That, or pretend that she's a firm believer in peer tutoring and has Michael, our seventh-grade resident math genius in the second row, explain the problem *and* the solution to the class. Which I never mind. I like his voice, the soft, soothing lilt of his accent. His family's from India, which is supposed to be a Third World country, but what I want to know is, if that country is supposed to be so poor and un-educated, how come Michael, who just came here last year, is so good at math? Good at everything, actually. He gets straight A's, but in math . . . that's where he really shines.

"Carla wrote a check for the full cost," Ms. Harris says. "Show how she wrote the amount in words and in numbers on the check."

Easy-peasy, as the Naked Chef on TV would say. I bend over my paper. I've got a competition going with myself. Want to see if I can come up with the solution faster than Michael can. Not that he knows about this competition, it's not like we talk or anything. It's not like we're friends. It's just something I've made up to keep things interesting. I add $179.49 to $179.49 and get $358.98. I glance over at Michael, who seems to be already on the written part of it. Darn! I write as fast as I can. There, finished. I glance over again and Michael's looking out the window. Damn! Maybe next time. I stretch out my fingers, get in ready position. Wonder if it would be cheating if I started writing down the problem as Ms. Harris read it out, didn't wait for her to finish. I mean, if you want to get techni-cal, I could start the whole set right now. Do the whole thing, don't need her to explain it, I've got it right in front of me. Yeah, I think that would hold up in a court of law. This stuff is pretty self-explanatory, and if Michael wants to wait for her to read it, that's his choice!

If I was a bad guy in a movie, I'd chortle out loud.

I start solving problems like a math junkie gone wild. Problems and solutions flying out of the tip of my pencil. Michael's still gazing out of the window, has no idea that he is about to lose his "Math King" throne.

At his garage sale, Bryan priced comic books at twenty for one dollar, I read. *He wrote the price on each comic book as five cents. Is this correct? Explain.* Duh!

I'm about to answer it when suddenly I get this really bad pain. A lightning bolt, an electricity jolt erupting in the lower right base of my skull between my ear and my spine, shooting in an upward trajectory to explode out of my forehead, just above my left eyebrow. And then the pain gets so unbelievably intense that I have to fly my hands up to my head, grab a hold of it tight, and wrap my arms around it or it will burst into a million pieces, splatter the room, the walls, Sara's new shirt with brain particles. Someone's screaming. A high-pitched scream, and I'm not sure, but I think it might be me.

And that's it. I feel my body tumbling, and the darkness takes me.

● ● ● ●

When I come to, I am lying on the floor, sort of half under my desk. It's pretty gross under here. I had no idea how much chewed-up gum could be stuck under one desk. Years and years of it. Probably more graying gum than desk. I hear voices, people crowding around. Ms. Harris yelling, "Get back! Stand back, everybody! Give her air. Derek, run down to the office, get the nurse! Quick!"

I'm kind of embarrassed to be sprawled out on the floor. I'd like to get up, but when I try to move, Ms. Harris says, "Stay right where you are. Don't move."

"But I'm fine now," I say. "Really, I'm fine." And I am. The bad, bad pain is gone. Just a headache now. A dull ache all over, like somebody pounded on my head with a sledgehammer, not the fall-down excruciating pain of before. But she makes me stay on the floor. I feel like a fool. I really don't want to keep looking at the bottom of my desk, but I suppose it's better than having to sit up and look at my classmates. How humiliating.

The nurse comes. She asks me a few questions, feels my head. "Does this hurt? Does this?" I lie and say, "No, everything's fine." She has me get up, her pudgy arm around me for support. We're going to go to the sickroom. I keep my eyes down. I never have to go to the sickroom. Never! It's a source of pride, my resilience and good health. I never let a flu or a fever get me down. I'm not a sissy. My friend Emily comes with me, holding up my other side because my legs are feeling pretty shaky. I'm kind of wobbly. I don't look at Emily, but I can see her out of the corner of my eye, all pale-faced and concerned. How embarrassing.

● ● ● ●

My dad comes to me in my sleep.

My mom made me go to bed right when I got home. The school called and told her what had happened. She brought chicken soup and crackers up to my bedroom on a tray, even though I kept telling her that I was fine, wasn't sick.

I don't remember falling asleep, but when I wake up it's dark outside and the whole house is silent. And there my dad is, at the foot of my bed. I'm not scared or anything. Just happy to see him. It feels right that he's there, even though he's supposed to be on the other side of the world, living in a tent, keeping the peace. We talk about this and that, school and stuff. He's sitting on my bed, one leg swung over the other like he always does, but the bed's not indenting, and he's wearing his camouflage gear and Dad never wears that at home. That's how I know I'm just dreaming, but I don't care. I'm happy to stay in the dream and hang out with him. Wish he'd do really cool things like take me out the window and fly. Now that would be neat! But we don't. He tells me to take care of my brother and sister. Then he gives me a smile, does a vanishing trick with a coin, and when the coin disappears, he's gone too.

And then I'm awake, half-sitting in my bed. Not sure when I woke up, but here I am, and I can feel the night breeze from the cracked-open window on my face. The moon casts shadows across my bed. I wonder where he is now. My dad. Missing him so much that my throat is all constricted and sore, like I'd been crying loud, ragged sobs all night, but I haven't been. It's probably just the dream making me feel this way.

I snuggle down in bed, shut my eyes, and slow my breath. I try to trick my body into thinking it's asleep. If I keep my dad drifting, hovering in my thoughts, maybe he'll come to me in a dream again and this time take me flying.

● ● ● ●

I get dressed right when I wake up. I don't want to hang out in my pajamas like I usually do on weekend mornings. Don't know why. I can't explain the need, but it's like there was something about the taste, the quality of the air around me when I woke up that made me realize it was essential that I be up, dressed, and ready to go.

I head downstairs.

Tessa and Simon are sitting on the sofa, gawking bug-eyed at the TV.

"Anybody want some Lucky Charms?" I say. There is the obligatory TV-watching three-second delay, and then Tessa says, "Uh-huh" and Simon says, "Yeah, please." I get three bowls, three tablespoons, tuck the box of Lucky Charms under my arm. Normally I'd make Tessa move her butt off the sofa and get her own, but last night's dream is still lingering in my mind. I snag the milk from the fridge. Two percent. Don't know why Mom won't buy whole milk. It tastes so much better, probably a dieting thing. Mom's always watching her weight.

I go back out to the living room. Serve up Simon's cereal, not too much milk because he has a tendency to spill things. Once Simon's taken care of, I pour another and hand it off to Tessa. I set up my own bowl and sit down beside them.

They are watching *Rugrats*, one of Simon's favorites. Tessa pretends she's above it, that it's too babyish for her, but I notice that whenever Simon's watching it, there she is, sitting on the sofa beside him, soaking it up. It's a cute show. Harmless. I'll even watch it myself, now and then.

Simon's wearing his Spider-Man pajamas, and a pair of my old gym socks with a hole in one toe are hanging off his feet like flippers. Tessa's in her Beauty and the Beast nightgown that we got last year at Disney World. It's not that old, but it's worn thin because she wears it so much. It's pink, of course. Both of them have lopsided, sleep-squished hair, and then there's me, dressed and ready to go.

We munch away at our cereal, lined up on the sofa like the three little bears, watching cartoons. Chuckie's lost his dream and he's got the other Rugrats looking for it. Simon is laughing, Tessa too. There's a knock at the door. Not a rat-a-tat-tat "friend at the door" knock. It's a different kind of knock, hesitant but heavy. And I don't know why, but I don't want to answer it. It's funny how the Rugrats think you can just find a dream like that, looking under things, behind doors.

Knock . . . knock . . . knock. There it is again. Can't move. Stuck there, eyes hot, mouth dry, sitting on the sofa.

Simon scoots down to the edge of the sofa, climbs off, and I can see the wrinkled imprint from his bedsheet on his face. And there is something about that imprint that makes him seem even more vulnerable than usual. His dark-chocolate hair flops forward, and he brushes it off his face with a sleepy fist, eyes still on the TV, on Tommy, Phil, Lil, and Chuckie looking for Chuckie's dream.

Simon starts to head to the front door, but I grab his arm quick, before he can get very far. I'm scared. Don't want to go myself, but I don't want him to answer the door either. Not looking like this, with his sweet, puppy-dog innocence.

"But, Jack," he says, looking confused. "Someone's at the door." Lisping slightly because he has a loose tooth on the bottom and doesn't like his tongue scraping against it.

"So what? That's not our problem. We're watching Chuckie." Like I care about this stupid cartoon. "Just because somebody comes to the door," I explain, my voice practical and calm, even though I'm sweating all over, "doesn't mean we have to leap up and get it. They'll just have to come back later."

"Why, Jack?" he says, head tipping to the side. "Why don't you want me to answer the door?"

"I just *don't*, that's all!" My patience is suddenly gone. I know I sound grouchy, but I don't care.

So he sits back down, eyes big. Doesn't answer the door. Tessa neither, because I'm the oldest. I'm in charge. Someone knocks again. I grab the remote control, turn the TV volume up way loud, and we sit there. Tessa and Simon watching the show, like obedient little zombies, and me, I'm keeping my head facing toward the TV too, but my eyes are sideways, watching the two soldiers through the window, standing on the front step, hats in their hands. One of them is twirling his hat nervously. And I know what they're here for, on our steps, in formal dress.

A commercial comes on, a blond-haired, blue-eyed girl playing with some kind of princess Barbie and so, obviously, Tessa's transfixed.

The taller man in his stiff, starched uniform knocks again. Quite loudly this time. I can hear the sound of his fist hitting the wood over the blaring TV.

"Why are you crying, Jack?" Simon asks, resting his hand on my arm, a worried look on his face.

And that's when Mom comes storming through the living room. "For God's sake, children!" Yanking on her pale-blue terry-cloth robe, tying the belt in an angry knot around her middle, the rest of the robe trying to catch up, billowing behind her like it's caught in a windstorm, legs striding forward, body too, bent slightly at the waist. She is yelling at all of us, but her enraged eyes focus on me, like it's all my fault.

"Is it too much to ask? For you to *answer* the door! Jeez! One of my rare days to sleep in, and you can't be bothered!"

And she's really mad, otherwise I'd tell her not to answer the door too. But she does. She opens it and hears what the soldiers on the steps have to say.

● ● ● ●

We don't go trick-or-treating. None of us feel like it. We don't give out candy either, don't have the heart to answer the door, act like everything's okay. Like our dad hasn't just been killed by "friendly fire," whatever the hell that means!

We don't feel like smiling pretty, handing out candy, admiring little pirates and fairy princesses. Don't feel like carousing through the darkened streets ourselves, stuffing our pillowcases, our stomachs with candy. It wouldn't feel right. So we have an early dinner, stay home, close the curtains, turn off the lights, sit in the dark, don't answer the door. Just sit there listening to everybody outside, running up and down the street, shrieks and laughter, "Trick-or-treat!" and "Oh my! Look at you!" A few kids who don't know any better knock on our door, even though it's obvious we aren't home. Our lights are out, duh! Anyway, finally they go away, but they come back and pelt our door with eggs and rotten old tomatoes. Guess they hadn't heard about our dad.

When I get up in the morning, I have a heck of a time washing the stuff off. Have to take the scrub brush to it because part of the goo hardened overnight. Some people are real jerks.

● ● ● ●

SPRING

Starting up the walkway to our house, I get one of those feelings again. Not bad like when Dad died, but a feeling nonetheless. A reluctance in the pit of my stomach, don't know why, just know I don't want to go inside. Not yet.

"Hey, Simon," I say. "How about I give you a push on the swing first, before we start our homework?" "Okay," he says, because if there's one thing Simon hates, it's homework and school. He's having a real tough time with reading and printing, can't even spell his name without help. And I worry because he doesn't seem to have progressed at all this year. It's probably the trauma of losing our dad that's making him get so far behind in school. Making him have to come in my bedroom every night, his small face pale from bad dreams, needing to crawl in bed with me in order to sleep. One arm flung over me for safety, so I can't disappear in the night. And I lie there all stiff, not wanting to move. He needs his sleep.

Spring

We go around the side of the house with its peeling white paint, chapped and roughened like a fisherman's hands. Bits and particles ripped off by the wind. The brown sludge squishes under our feet. Used to be pretty, our yard. Small, but pretty and well kept. Neat. Almost don't recognize it, walking up sometimes, that this is our house, our yard. All derelict and abandoned-looking. It's weird how fast things can let go. Slide wrong.

Ever since Mom got the bad news, everything fell apart. She's like a dress that hasn't been stitched, the bits of fabric just laid out on the table and a strong wind, a slammed door, could tumble her away.

And, yes, it's sad. I miss my dad awful, but there comes a point where you've got to pull your bootstraps up, because we're closing in on April and Mom's still crying. It's like she became a puddle of a person. Stopped going to work, just went to bed, and that was it. No more mother.

The refrigerator's out of food and the freezer too. Sometimes I can get Mom up and out of bed. Get her to the store so we can use her credit card on some groceries, but sometimes no. And then it's peanut butter and crackers for us kids because that's all that's left. And now, as if we don't have enough troubles, there's something weird about the house. I can't put my finger on it, but something's off.

I get Simon going on the swing. Then I go inside.

Everything seems okay. Nice and quiet. Mom's not on one of her lost binges, screaming and laughing and crying all at once, hair matted, fingernails ripping her face. That's what I was worried about, so that's good.

"Mom?" I say, my voice echoing slightly in the empty kitchen. "Mom?" I check out the living room. All clear. The bathroom. Everything's fine. There's a new stack of official-looking envelopes stuffed through the mail slot in the front door. Most of them with *Immediate Attention Required* stamped in red ink across them. I pick them up, open the closet door, toss them on top of all the other mail Mom keeps in there, up on the shelf above the hangers and coats. Most of them stay up because I've become pretty expert at this, but some of the envelopes slither down. Too much overflow. She'll have to find a new storage place soon. I shove the rogue envelopes into the closet with my toe and shut the door.

I go back out to the living room. There's an empty gap where our TV, VCR, and DVD player used to sit. Dad's stereo is gone too. That happened last week, along with the coffee table. These men just came in and took it all. Mom standing there in her robe, fiery patches on her cheeks, arms hanging loosely at her sides. They took her fancy vanity dresser with the circular mirror, her wood bedframe and matching side table, the kitchen table and chairs. Simon went crazy, kicking and biting at the men. I had to pull him off. I was scared one of those big guys would lose his temper and slug him, but they just disappeared their big, beefy heads down into the collars of their shirts, their thick necks and tips of their ears turning red. Blinking eyes, shut faces, looking right through us kids like we were air.

I'm just about to go upstairs and check out the bedrooms before I'll let Simon come in when it hits me. I know what's wrong. It's too quiet. Abnormally quiet. Not just because Mom isn't going crazy again. It's a deeper kind of quiet. No inside sound at all, just Simon's voice whooping on the swing and Tessa's light voice rising above his boisterous boy noises like a flute.

"Oh good," I say. "Tessa got home." She had stayed late to finish decorating her Ukrainian Easter egg.

I flip the light switch. Nothing. Could be the bulb is burnt out. I go back to the kitchen and stand in the doorway. I try that switch too. Nothing. The numbers on the stove clock aren't right either, they're stuck on 11:47. I go over to the stove anyway, turn on the front right burner. Nothing. Doesn't turn glowing red, no heat, even though I wait for a while with my outstretched palm not more than an inch away from the coil. And that's when I realize why it's so still. The fridge isn't humming and neither is the furnace.

I go over to the heat registers along the baseboards of the floor, put my hand on them. Nothing. No heat, just cold metal, and all of a sudden I feel chilled through and through, like I'm in an ice-cube bath and I'll never be warm again.

I run back to the living room, look out the big plate-glass window at all the other houses, hoping against hope. But no such luck. The power lines aren't down. There are house lights on in the other houses up and down the street.

"Mom!" I call, banging on her bedroom door. "Mom!" But the door is locked and she doesn't come out. Apparently she can't hear me, even though Simon and Tessa playing in the backyard have no problem with their ears. They hear me perfectly well. Come running, out of breath, windswept hair.

"What is it, Jack? What is it?" And I don't know what to say. I don't know what to tell them. So I take them back outside and have them swing some more.

● ● ● ●

I'm in the middle of a spelling test when the principal, Ms. Campbell, announces over the PA: "Will Jacqueline, Tessa, and Simon Cooper please report to the office. Jacqueline, Tessa, and Simon Cooper. Thank you." And everybody goes, "Ohhh, you're in trouble!" But I don't think I am because I haven't done anything wrong that I know of, and besides, she's called my little brother and sister to the office too.

I meet up with Tessa coming out of Ms. Beaufort's class. She looks scared, walking small. She tries to slip her hand in mine, but I shrug her off, stuff my hands in my pockets before she gets any more crazy ideas. I mean, come on! I might be nervous too, but I'm *not* about to walk down the hall holding hands with my sister. We walk past the "I can read!" first-grade bulletin board with all its bright colors and happy streamers. Poor Simon, he *so* wanted his name on that board last year.

"What do you think it is?" Tessa whispers.

"I don't know." I shrug like its no big deal. My mouth is dry. We walk past the trophy case and there we are, right outside the office door. I turn the metal knob and push the door open. Tessa and I walk inside.

Mrs. Spingle is behind the counter, at her desk typing. "Go on in, you two," she says, gesturing at Ms. Campbell's door, her large, chunky bangles, red and blue, rattling.

I walk over, Tessa crowding close behind. The door is open a crack, so I give a knock and then push it open the rest of the way.

The principal is sitting at her desk, another lady's there too. She's standing, looking out the window. I don't recognize her at first. Been so long since I've seen Mom up and about wearing something other than her robe.

"Ms. Campbell?" I say.

"Hi, kids!" Mom turns, faces us wearing a lightbulb-bright smile. Her hair's brushed. She's got makeup on. Even lipstick.

"Where's Simon?" As if on cue, Simon appears at the doorway. He looks scared.

"Mom?" he says, and then it's like his short little legs take on a life of their own. They run him to her. His arms fling around her, hugging her tight, face buried in her skirt like she's been gone for years.

"Why are you here?" I ask Mom. Don't know why I feel so cautious, angry almost.

"I need you kids to go get your coats, backpacks, and stuff. We're going on a little trip. A family emergency has come up. Your great-grandmother needs us."

"Our great-grandmother?" And I'd say more, but Ms. Campbell is listening.

"Who?" says Tessa. "Who? What? Where are we going?"

"To see your great-grandmother, sweetheart, the one in Alberta." Mom smiles at Tessa like that explains everything.

"Alberta?" I say. "*Alberta!* Isn't that . . . on the other side of Canada?"

"Yes," Simon pipes up. "Alberta's beside Saskatchewan. The only province farther away is British Columbia."

"You've got to be kidding me!" I can't believe this. I really can't.

"No," Simon says earnestly. "I'm telling the truth. Isn't that right, Ms. Campbell?"

I don't wait for Ms. Campbell to answer. "How long are we

going for?" I ask Mom. I don't like the look she's got on her face and I don't know who the hell this "great-grandmother" is that she's babbling about.

"Oh, a week, two weeks, who knows? Depends on the circumstances, how fast she recovers."

"How fast . . . she *recovers?*" I can't believe my ears, this bullshit she's spinning.

"Yes," Mom chirps, "recovers . . . recovers . . ." waving her hands like that explanation should answer any questions.

"I'm so sorry, children," Ms. Campbell says. "I'll say a prayer for her this Sunday."

"But I have a math test tomorrow," I say, because, to be honest, this is just baloney and someone needs to inject a little sanity into this discussion. "We can't just go tromping off to Alberta. I can't miss my math test. It's really important, Mom!"

"I'll speak to your teacher, Jacqueline," Ms. Campbell's competent voice cuts in. "We'll work something out. Don't worry, dear." Her voice is so kindly. If only she knew. "Your great-grandmother's recovery is the important thing now."

So that's that. We go back to our classes, get our stuff, everybody asking, "What's going on?" "Where are you going?" "Oh, lucky!"

I speak with Ms. Harris and she lets me take my textbooks so I won't fall behind. She says I can take the math test, and any other tests I miss, when I get back.

Everybody's jealous that I'm going to miss school. But this is *not* a happy thing. Something doesn't feel right. Smells fishy. Why would Mom travel all the way to Alberta just because an imaginary "great-grandmother" is sick? We don't even have a grandmother, let alone a *great* one. And even if we did, why meet her now, in the middle of the school year? It doesn't make sense.

We gather in the parking lot at the back of the school. The trunk is full of our clothes, thrown in there willy-nilly, great armloads of clothes. No suitcases. Tessa and Simon's back-packs fit in fine, because neither one of them thought to take schoolwork. Mine doesn't, though. I have to ride with my feet propped up on it like a footrest.

Mom's vibrating. Practically ricocheting around the car. I have to unroll the window a crack.

"We're going on a va*cay*shun!" she sings. "A little va*cay*-shun!" All glittery and bright, like fool's gold. Tessa and Simon join in. "We're going on a va*cay*shun! A little va*cay*shun!" They sing, but I don't. I can't. I sit in the front seat, head tipped back against the headrest. I feel nauseous. Like everything's happening too fast. Eyes shut, arms crossed so nothing else bad can come in.

We're driving through town when Mom slams on the brakes. She's not a very good driver. It's a good thing someone invented seatbelts, otherwise us kids would be walking around with a lot of windshield glass permanently embedded in our heads. "Get out, get out," Mom says. Now normally, if my mom said, "Get out of the car," I would. No questions asked. But she's acting so weird that for a second the old Hansel and Gretel story flashes through my head, and I'm thinking she's going to ditch us here.

"Why?" I say, heart pounding. "We want to stay here."

"I'll get out," says suckhole Tessa, springing from the car like a smiley kid in a commercial, and once she's on the sidewalk, Simon follows suit and I have no choice. There's no way I'm going to leave Tessa and Simon alone with Mom right now. Not with her acting so crazy.

"Okay, kids," Mom says, rummaging in her purse, getting her powder compact out, opening it up, blotting away the shine on her forehead and nose. "I want you to look sad-eyed and hungry. Can you do that?"

Sad-eyed and hungry? "Why?" I say, but she's already on the move. "Why, Mom?"

"I might get a better price. Shush . . . shush. Here we are." She puts on a smile and pushes open the door. There is an electronic bell that buzzes as we come in. I've never been in this store. Lived in St. John's all my life, never knew it existed. It's a real mishmash of things. Guitars, a drum set, video cameras, jewelry. Anything you could think of, this store's got. Mom walks up to the glass counter. They've got watches in there and fancy earrings and necklaces. The greasy-haired man behind the counter hoists himself off his stool, ambles over. He's got a cigarette dangling from his lips, which is dropping ashes on the floor. Smoking. Doesn't care if there's kids in his store. He doesn't care that cigarette smoke is bad for our lungs, he's smoking anyway. Wish my dad was here. He'd give him what for.

Mom slides her gold wedding ring and her diamond engagement ring, with the gold leaves that hold the diamond up, off of her finger.

"What are you doing, Mom?" I ask, stomach feeling tight. She ignores me. Takes the matching diamond studs out of her earlobes. The earrings Dad had saved for. Cradles them in the palm of her hand.

"What will you give me for these?" she asks.

The man reaches behind him, gets a little black magnifying glass that fits over one eye. Examines the rings and the earrings, turning them over with his dirt-encrusted hands. Filthy. Like he's never heard of soap and water. He hocks up a chunk of phlegm from the base of his throat, swishes it around his mouth like it's mouthwash, swallows, tosses the earrings and the rings back in Mom's hand. "Two hundred and fifty. Take it or leave it."

"Two hundred and fifty," Mom says weakly.

"Mom!" I say. "Don't do it! The guy's ripping you off!"

"Stay out of it, Jacqueline," Mom says, voice sharp.

"No! Dad paid twelve hundred for the earrings alone. Twelve hundred dollars! He showed me the receipt, and that's *just* for the earrings. I don't even know what the fancy diamond ring cost him, or your wedding ring."

"Jacqueline!" Mom snaps. "Go to the car!"

"No!" I cry out. "I won't let you do it!"

"Five hundred even," the man says. "That's my last offer."

"I'll take it," Mom says, and the jewelry Dad gave her disappears in the man's grubby hand. He goes into the back room and comes out with a fistful of money. I would leave because I'm so pissed off at Mom, but I don't. Someone has to keep her head. I count out the money over Mom's shoulder to make sure the creep doesn't pull a fast one.

Back in the car, Mom's not mad at me anymore. She says I did good. She smiles at me like I backtalked her on purpose. Like it was my clever strategy to get more money out of him.

I let her go on thinking that. Why not? It's better than having her furious at me for opening up my fat yap.

And I'm grateful that I never told Mom about Dad giving me his watch. I knew it was a secret and kept it that way. I'm glad she didn't know that I had it under my shirt, hanging from a cowhide shoelace I knotted around my neck. My dad's watch resting right over my heart, where it should be, where my dad is. I only take it off if I'm going in the shower.

So I'm real glad I never told Mom, because that man had lots of watches behind his counter. A *lot* of watches, not half as nice as my dad's. And if my mom knew that I had Dad's watch, she probably would have made me sell that as well. The idea of losing Dad's watch makes my throat close up and my eyes burn hot. I tip my head back against the headrest and squeeze my eyes shut, but it doesn't help. The tightness in my throat won't let up, because no matter how hard I try, I can't get the image out of my mind of my dad's jewelry rolling around in that man's dirty hand.

● ● ● ●

Nobody's singing now. Even the arguing in the backseat has stopped, that's how tired out everybody is. Mom's gripping the steering wheel way too hard, like if she just wills it, the car will start behaving, stop overheating.

"I wanna go home," Tessa says.

"Shut up," I say because, really, any idiot can see that Mom's under enough stress as it is. We just need her to hold it together until we get to Alberta. If she comes unraveled now, we're lost. But I know what Tessa means. I woke up yesterday missing the view from my bedroom window, the tang of the salt air blown in off the ocean, missing it so bad it stung. The land here seems to stretch on forever, and the sky feels wider to me than the sky back home. It's not a comfortable feeling, all this wide-open space. Makes me feel small.

Three and a half days now we've been on the road, grit in our teeth. Catnaps at rest stops. Half-sleep, sometimes for an hour or two. Doors locked. Key in the ignition, always ready to move on if there's any sign of trouble. Mom and me, sleeping upright, seats tipped back just enough so our necks aren't always jerking our heads forward when sleep comes. Simon and Tessa in the backseat, flopped over each other, all arms and legs, like two baby cubs snuggled up together.

No motels or campgrounds on this road trip. It's not like when Dad was alive. We aren't having special treats at A&W or Tim Hortons. Everything's different. It's peanut butter and crackers or shut your yap. We ran out of the strawberry jam on Day Two. We've got three plastic jugs that we fill up at gas stations, rest stops, wherever has free water. One's for us to drink, the other two are for the radiator.

"Come on, baby," Mom whispers under her breath, pushing forward slightly, like she's a jockey on an old, tired racehorse. "Come on." I don't even know if she's aware that she's speaking. "You can do it. Come on." Several of the warning lights are lit up on her dashboard. I glance over at her gas gauge, but it seems to be fine, the arrow pointing a little over half a tank. I slide my eyes to the hood of the car. Everything seems fine there, no steam or smoke coming out. Shouldn't be. We just pulled over to the side of the road and refilled the radiator less than half an hour ago. I'm getting to be quite a radiator fixer-upper,

and I can tell you this new problem we're having has nothing
to do with the radiator.

"What's that noise, Mom?" Simon asks, sitting up abruptly.

"What noise?" I say.

"That noise," Simon says. "Can't you hear it?"

I listen hard. I can hear something. A crackling, kind of
popping sound. Sort of like somebody is tossing handfuls of
gravel at the bottom of the car.

"It's just gravel, Simon," I say.

"But we aren't on a gravel road. We're on a paved road.
How can it be gravel?"

"Hmm." He's got a point there. "Maybe there's some little
rocks that got tossed up on the road. Or maybe a dump truck
full of gravel passed this way and hit a bump, and some of his
gravel fell off the back of his truck onto the road, and now it's
spitting up onto the metal bottom of our car. Or maybe –"

"Kids, can you be quiet, please?" Mom says. "I've got a
headache." And I think she's telling the truth because her face
is all shadowed and drawn and she looks a little white around
the mouth. So I shut up.

That is, until I smell the smoke. Not a cozy, wood-burning
smoke that makes you think of a log fire in the winter or a hot-
dog roast in the fall. This is a different kind of smoke. A chem-
ical, electrical one.

"There's smoke, Mom," I say.

"What?"

"There's smoke. Stop the car!" Mom sniffs the air and smells it too. Starts screaming like a crazy woman, swerves to the side of the road. We jump out of the car. All the car doors go flying open at once, like a juice box that has been stomped on. Thick-fingered and fumbly, I get the hood open. It's hard to do because the metal's so hot, which is not a good sign. But I get it open, and sure enough when that dusty sky-blue metal top rises, I can see flames.

"Get back!" I yell to my little brother and sister. "Get back! Get to the other side of the road!" I've seen enough TV shows to know that if those flames get to the gas tank, this whole car could blow. And Mom? She's useless. She's just screaming, wringing her hands, and dancing around like she's gonna pee herself. I dive into the backseat and yank out the full plastic container. I grab the half-empty one too. I'm pulling off the red lids while I round the front of the car, dumping the water on the engine as soon as it's within reach. All that water hitting the hot engine is creating a huge, billowing cloud of steam. Makes it damned hard to see. I dump more water on, dousing the flames. I have to aim careful. Don't want to waste any. It's really touch-and-go, but I get that fire out. Don't have any water left, though. Nothing for the radiator, no drinking water for us either, and I could use a drink right now. My mouth is dry as last week's biscuits.

I turn around. "It's out," I say. My voice is kind of wobbly like it doesn't belong to me. "The fire's out."

When Mom hears that the fire's out, instead of being glad, her legs drop her down in the dirt by the side of the road and she starts crying, her body rocking back and forth. She looks like one of those women you see on TV documentaries that survived the war but everybody's dead and they're cursing God, wailing up at the sky. I want to say, "We're *here*, Mom! We're *not* all dead." But what good would that do? So I go in search of water. I bring both jugs. Not that anything I find will be okay for drinking, but we are going to need it, not just for the finicky radiator, but for the engine now as well.

● ● ● ●

I don't have to go far. About a quarter-mile down the road is a little creek. I dig at it with a stick to make a gully so the mouth of the jugs can get in the water. I manage to fill them halfway. I get on my hands and knees, bend down, and take a long drink, even though if my dad was around he'd probably kill me. "Just because it's water doesn't mean it's drinkable," he'd say. "You don't want to get yourself sick with beaver fever. You always have to boil it, or use one of these little doodads," he'd said once, waving his fancy camping water-purifying cup at me. "Got that?" And I did. But now, at this particular moment,

I don't care. I'm dying of thirst, and if drinking this water kills me, so be it.

When I get back to the car, my arms are about ready to fall off from the weight of the jugs. But Mom's stopped crying and Simon is snuggled up next to her and Mom's got her arm around Tessa, so that's good.

"Hey, Simon," I say, just like my dad did, using the same kind of voice. "Want to learn how to fill up the radiator?" And he leaps to his feet, the biggest smile on his face.

"Sure," he says, hiking up his jeans.

"See that there?" I say, pointing at the radiator cap, handing him the rag. "Now normally that baby is piping hot, so you only twist it open a little at a time, and you use this rag so you don't burn your hands." It's probably pointless to be teaching him this because from the way this engine looks, we aren't going to be driving anywhere any time soon.

"Someone's coming!" Tessa yells. We all look up to see a truck on the horizon. Mom runs over to the car, reaches inside and pushes a little button that makes all the car lights flash red, and we jump up and down waving our arms and yelling. Thank goodness the pickup truck slows down and stops.

"What seems to be the problem here?" the driver says out the window, pushing his frayed baseball cap back, giving the top of his head a scratch.

"Oh," Mom says, her words tumbling out. "We've just had the worst luck. The engine caught on fire, God knows why. It won't start up again and I don't know what to do. I've got these children, and my husband's dead and we've got to get to Alberta because we've got relatives there." He looks at her and she looks at him. I can tell Mom's trying to smile, keep a brave face on, but tears are almost ready to come again. I hope they don't because that would be really humiliating. I think he can tell that she might cry too because he pulls his truck to the side of the road, turns the engine off, and gets out.

He walks around our car and listens to Mom talk. It's like once she gets started, she can't stop, but he doesn't seem to mind. I think he likes it, actually, because it's like he's the big man, the hero in the movies, rescuing a woman in need. He listens as my mom's voice washes over him, scratches his head some more, and then pulls a rope out of the back of his truck.

When I first see the rope, I'm a little nervous because what if we read him wrong and he's going to tie us up and kidnap us? But he doesn't. Just flops on his back, scoots his head and chest under our car, knees bent facing up toward the sky, fiddles around under there. Doesn't seem to mind about the dirt. That's the kind of thing my dad would do. He didn't mind about dirt either. He would do what needed to be done, with no complaints.

The old guy slides out again, dirt clinging to the back of his shirt and his saggy jeans. He backs up his truck so the rear of it is almost touching the front bumper of our car. Then he takes the free end of the rope and uses it to attach our car to a big metal knob he has sticking out from under his pickup truck.

"Will that hold?" I say. I'm not being rude, I just want to make sure. I don't want the weight of our car to rip off the back of his truck and create damage we can't pay for, not to mention what would happen to our car as it went careening down the road with no driver at the wheel. Our car might be broken now, but at least we've got it. It's still good for sleeping in.

"Was made for this kinda situation," he says. His voice is scratchy dry, like an old played-out recording. He's got hair, though. A full head of it. Gray-blond strawlike tufts sticking up and out from his scalp in no particular order.

He opens our door and gets behind the wheel, starts fiddling around.

"What are you doing now?" Simon asks, eyes big, sparkling, like this is a great adventure.

"Simon," Mom says. "Let him be."

"It's okay, ma'am, I don't mind." He turns back to Simon. "You've got to put this thing in neutral, otherwise we're screwed," he grunts. He slides back out, straightens up, shuts the car door. Goes to the back of his truck, puts the rear flap down.

"You kids hop in," he says, giving the truck a pat, shifting the wad of stuff he's got in his cheek to the other side, turning his head slightly to the left. Brown spittle, shooting out between his teeth, leaves a trailing dribble on his prickly salt-and-pepper chin, which he wipes off with the back of his hand. "You, ma'am," he says, gesturing to Mom, "can ride in front."

"Thank you." She smiles graciously like he's just asked her to the ball, and when Mom smiles at him, I swear to God, this old guy turns beet red. Looks down at his boots. I almost expect him to say, "Garsh." Like Big Moose in the *Archie* comics.

"Holy cow!" Simon exclaims. "Did you see how far that went?" He's really impressed with this old guy's spitting abilities.

We scramble up into the back of his faded green pickup truck, all the seams rusting out, making our way around his tools and things as he shuts the rear flap and secures it. He's got some plastic bags of manure stacked along the back side that look like pretty good seats so we sit on them. Mom climbs in the front. He gives her a hand. "Thank you," she says, smiling at him again. "You've been so kind." This guy was red before, but it's nothing on what he is now. He couldn't get any redder.

So here we are, everything was going so bad, but now look how it turned out! I'm going to get my first ride in the back of a pickup truck. I've always wanted to do this, ride free with the wind in my hair, no seatbelt, just me and the open road.

"Hang on," I tell Tessa and Simon because the last thing I want is for this old guy to hit a bump and send them flying in the air. I make a show of grabbing on hard with both hands and they do the same.

"All ready back there?" the old guy calls out his window, giving another spit for good measure. And I hope he doesn't intend to spit all the way into town, because who knows where the wind is going to send it.

"A-okay!" I yell back all cheerful as he turns the engine over and shifts into gear. "Keep your mouths closed," I say, leaning over to Tessa and Simon. I don't say this too loud because I don't want to hurt the old guy's feelings.

"Why?" Simon says, but I can't go into the logistics of flying spit. No telling how good this guy's hearing is.

"Just do it!" I give them both a look so they know I mean business. Their mouths snap shut quicker than a Venus flytrap.

The guy pulls out on the road, nice and gentle. He doesn't take it too fast, and sure enough, our car follows. When I twist around I can see the back of Mom through the rearview window. She's talking up a storm, her hands waving around. The old guy is just nodding every now and then, maybe an "Uh-huh," but that seems to be it. I can't tell. It's impossible to hear anything with the wind in my ears and that's fine with me. I just want to enjoy the ride. Just want to enjoy the feeling of almost flying, the afternoon air blasting my face and my hair.

● ● ● ●

The old guy's brother has a mechanic shop. It's a weather-beaten shed with two gas pumps outside. One is for regular fuel and one is for diesel. Ed and his brother look quite similar. Only difference is, Ed's wiry skinny and Ed's brother, Dick, is skinny with a little potbelly hanging over his rodeo belt. And already I can tell another difference: as little as Ed talks, that's how much Dick does. He's a real chatty guy.

"What the hell you do here?" Dick asks my mom.

"I don't know," Mom says. "I really don't know. The little lights on the dashboard kept on flashing, but I didn't know what they meant. My husband used to take care of the car, the house maintenance, things like that . . ." I hope she's not going to start crying again.

Dick doesn't notice, though. He's got his head under the hood, doing a run-through. "Out of oil. Clean out of oil. This car here is dry as a bone," he says, whistling through his teeth, shaking his head like somebody just shot his dog.

"It is?" Mom says. She looks so lost and unsure. "Oil? Was . . . was I supposed to be putting that in there? I mean, I knew about gas . . . but oil?"

"Yes, ma'am. You've got to check your oil regular as rain. See this little domahhicky? When you fill up the car with gas-o-lean, you've got to take this here thingamajig out, wipe it on an old rag or a paper towel." He demonstrates. "And then you stick it back in here, all the way down, take it out again. That's how you check the oil levels. See this?" He points to a little nick in the metal.

I can sort of see from where I'm standing that there's something printed on it, but I'm not close enough to see what and I don't want to crowd them. I make a note in my head where he puts the oil stick back. I'll get a good look later tonight. That way I'll know what to do.

"When the oil is below this line, this is where you say to yourself, 'Hmm, I think I need to buy some oil.' Now look what you got yourself here. What do you see? Nothing. No oil to be had. That's why your car caught on fire. Had no lubricant. Nothing to help the car to run smooth, metal rubbing against metal. That's what happened, little lady. That's what happened."

"Is it fixable?" Mom asks, face pale and eyes scared.

"Um . . . hum."

"How much will it cost? I . . . I don't have much." Her voice soft, ashamed. "And we . . . we still have to get to Wheatonville."

"Um . . . hum," Ed's brother says. They take a look at us, Ed and Dick. They size up the situation, how things are, what Mom's got in her wallet without her even taking it out of her purse.

"I'll just charge you the cost of the parts. How's that? Won't charge you for labor."

"How much will that be?"

"Not much . . . Not much."

"What if . . . I don't have enough?" Mom says, embarrassed. So embarrassed.

"You can owe me. I'll give you my address. You can send the balance when you get yourself and your kids set up."

Mom looks like she's going to cry. "Thank you," she says. "Both of you. I can't tell you what this means."

Ed and Dick put a folding chair out in the shade for Mom. Ed takes out a key from the bottom of the cash register and opens up the soda machine. He lets us kids each choose a free soda. I get cherry Coke, ice-cold and good. It's been so long since we've had pop and Mom gets one too. Sprite. It's a nice and peaceful time, Ed and Dick working on the car, the transistor radio by the till playing country-and-western songs. Drinking our sodas, drawing designs in the dirt with sticks, tic-tac-toe, that kind of thing, and when we get tired of that, we run in the field out back behind the garage. And when a customer comes, I try to help out, wash the windows, check the oil because I can do that now. Ed showed me how.

● ● ● ●

We've pulled to the side of the road for the night. Nobody around for miles, just fields and trees and an enormous night sky.

"What does our great-grandmother look like?" Tessa's voice pipes up from the backseat floor. She's using our backpacks and a layer of clothes to try to level out the hump in the middle. She thinks she's going to sleep there, but my money's on her getting tired of it in twenty minutes and crawling back up on the backseat she shares with Simon.

"Old," says Mom, like that's the end of the conversation. She's tired. I can tell. This trip has taken its toll on her.

"No, Mom, you know what I mean! Of *course* she's old, she's *your* grandmother. But what's she look like other than that? Does she have light hair like you and me? Or dark brown, more like Jack and Simon? What color are her eyes?"

"I don't know. I don't remember."

"You don't remember?" Tessa says. "How could you not remember? She's your grandmother."

Mom doesn't answer.

"Did you like her? Was she nice?"

Mom doesn't answer those questions either.

"Are we going to meet our grandparents too?" Simon asks.

"No, stupid!" Tessa snorts. "They're dead."

"I'm not stupid!" Simon says.

"Yes, you are!"

"No, he's not, Tessa," I butt in.

"But Mom told us . . ."

"He doesn't remember."

"I don't . . . remember," Simon says in a woebegone voice. "What happened? When did they die?"

"A long time ago," Mom says.

"Did I know them?"

"No, Simon," Mom says.

"Did Jack meet them? Or Tessa?"

"No, Simon . . . *Jeez!*" Tessa erupts. "Don't you *ever* listen? They were in a car crash, *okay?* They died when Mom was twelve. So *I* didn't meet them. *Jack* didn't meet them. *You* didn't meet them. *None* of us met them. I don't know why you've got to go on like that when you know perfectly well what happened!"

I'd say something to Simon, but it might set Tessa off again. And anyway, Mom's pretty fragile from Dad dying and all, so I don't think discussing the sudden death of her two parents is really a good idea.

"I didn't know," Simon finally says. "What did you do?"

There is a long pause, then Mom says, "I had to go live with my grandpa and gran."

"Our great-grandmother?"

"Yes, your great-grandmother."

"Do we have a great-grandpa too?" Simon asks.

"No. He's passed on."

"How come we've never met her?" Tessa asks, joining in.

"She lived too far away," Mom says, but I'm in the front seat, and out of the corner of my eye I can see that her face is saying something else.

"We've met Nonnie," Tessa says. "Daddy's mom, and she lived far away. She lived all the way in Manitoba and we went to see her every summer and she came to see us too. And Manitoba's a long way away."

"I miss Nonnie." Simon's plaintive voice drifts over the backseat. "I wish she didn't have to die."

"Nonnie was very old, Simon," Mom says. She sounds so tired. "Very sick. It was a relief for her . . . to finally let go." I glance over at Mom, and I wonder if she wants to let go too. I can't see much, just her profile, head leaned back, eyes shut. Beyond the dusty glass window is the night sky, and I make myself think about that instead of Mom. There is a barbed-wire fence around the perimeter of a freshly plowed field. And I wonder if it has just been planted, or if it is waiting to be. Rows and rows of rich dark dirt, stretching on for what seems to be forever. The stench of freshly laid fertilizer makes the air heavy around us. My mind turns back to Mom losing both her parents at my age, and I think about Nonnie too. Then the thought of my dad flashes before me, that he's dead and gone. Buried deep in the ground. I try not to think about it, but my mind goes there anyway. What does he look like now? And images flicker, like they always do, of maggots chewing him away, crawling in and out of his body. Does he have eyeballs left? Or empty, staring sockets?

I don't share my thoughts with the rest of the car.

I force my mind to delete that image of him. Try to picture his smiling, laughing face instead.

I miss him so much.

There are night sounds all around. Night creatures, scuttling, burrowing, getting ready for tomorrow. Nearby, the sudden flap of wings, the harsh cry of a bird. Our breath, our thoughts, beating against the confines of the car.

"What's our great-grandmother like, Mom?" Tessa won't give it a break. Mom sighs.

"You'll see tomorrow," she finally says. "You'll see tomorrow."

● ● ● ●

We get up early. We always do, so no one will discover us parked on the side of the road, living out of the car, throw stones at us, tell us to "Move along." The night sky just starting to streak with light, incoherent dark shapes becoming finely etched silhouettes. Morning is coming.

We tumble our bodies out of the car and rub, slap our arms, dance slightly, jiggling from foot to foot to keep warm. We take turns going to the other side of the car, into the ditch, squatting down to relieve ourselves. Our bare feet, our calves get wet from the early-morning dew clinging to the sleepy blades of green grass, making everything so pretty. Even the barbed-wire fence has a row of shimmering droplets, hanging like diamond jewels. Decorating a scrub brush with just the beginning of pale-green tips, tiny baby buds starting to form along the branches. All tucked up tight inside themselves, not sure if the harsh, cold winter is really over.

We are up, and the morning birds are too. A slew of them arcing over our heads, landing a good thirty yards away to feast on bugs, worms, and insects in the freshly dug field. They cry greetings to one another, fighting over the supposed best spots. I can see my warm breath rolling out of my mouth, like fog on the water, and then disappearing, joining the rest of the air.

I stretch my arms up high above my head. Simon glances over and copies me.

Today is the day we finally meet our great-grandmother. I hope she's not too sick. Mom was pretty vague on the drive here as to what her gran has. Hope it's nothing too serious, not like what Nonnie had. Hope it's just a false alarm, something mild, so we can meet her, have a meal or two, and then turn around and go back home. I don't want to get too far behind in my schoolwork.

After everybody's stretched a bit and had a pee, I flip up the hood of the car. I top up the radiator with water and check the oil. I stare at everything else for a while. I don't know what I'm looking at really. Just figure it can't hurt to give it a good hard look down the end of my nose, so it will know who it's dealing with, I'm not fooling around, I'm my father's daughter.

I slam the hood down all businesslike, sling the water container into its spot on the backseat floor, wipe my hands off on my jeans, hop in the front seat, and shut the door.

"Ready to go," I say, strapping in. Mom pulls out, the car coughing a bit, clearing its throat, and we're on our way.

● ● ● ●

It doesn't take long to get to our great-grandmother's house. Not more than an hour, an hour and a half. I was kind of surprised, seeing as how close it was, that Mom didn't just drive us there last night. We could have slept in a warm house, maybe even in a bed.

Another weird thing is we were all looking at the numbers on the mailboxes that appear every now and then along the road. When we passed the number that Mom was looking for and called it out, Mom just kept on driving. Didn't even slow down. So now here we are, soaring along the road, going away from the place that we drove all this way to get to.

"Mom! Mom!" we're all yelling. "We passed it! We passed it, Mom! That was it! Thirteen fifty-eight! That was it, we passed it!" But Mom keeps on driving like she's deaf, dumb, and blind. Keeps on driving a good five to ten minutes, even though now we're up in the fourteen hundreds. Mom's cheeks are a blazing forest-fire red. Her neck too, all the way down to where it disappears into the collar of her shirt.

When Mom finally stops the car, she gets out, clutching her belly. She bends over like she's got to throw up, but she doesn't. Nothing comes up but air. We stay in the car, strapped in, facing forward, like we're still sailing down the road in the wrong direction.

When Mom finishes getting rid of nothing, she returns to the car, wiping her mouth on the back of her wrist. She gets in, sits in the car. Her hands on the wheel. She doesn't turn the key in the ignition, though. Just sits there.

We don't say anything. Not even Tessa.

I don't know how long we sit there. Nobody talking, just the sound of our breath.

"Children," Mom finally says, pushing the strands of hair that have fallen forward away from her face. Her voice is ragged, weary. "Your great-gran isn't sick. I lied. She doesn't know we're coming. She doesn't even know you exist." Then Mom starts the car, pulls slowly out into the packed dirt and gravel road, and turns the car around. "So I'm going to need you to co-operate. I want you to be on your best behavior. Help out in the kitchen, with the housework, help with the chores. Do you understand?" Mom asks, swinging her head round to look at me, then back at Tessa and Simon.

"Yes, Mom," we say in unison, like we're doing a call-and-response song.

"I'm telling you. I'm serious about this. Your great-gran is old school. Do you know what that means?"

"No, Mom."

"It means *no* backtalk. You especially, Jacqueline. I want 'yes, please' and 'no, thank-you' every time. Good manners, no elbows on the table, children are meant to be seen, not heard. You understand me?"

"Yes, Mom."

"If she asks you to do something, you do it. No complaints. Do I make myself clear?"

"Oh God." Mom says this to herself, under her breath. I doubt Simon and Tessa even hear. "I hope she still lives there . . . Hasn't died . . . moved."

"Why did you say she was sick?" I ask.

"Shut up! No questions! You be polite, young lady, and do as you're told!"

So I shut up. Not another peep out of me, or any of us. Just the sound of the tires on the road.

We don't have to call out when Mom reaches the old, dented metal mailbox with thirteen fifty-eight stuck on it in square numbers made out of black tape. She pulls right into that old driveway like she's been doing it for years.

The driveway's bumpy, full of potholes. Mom tries to dodge

the worst ones. We round a slight curve, a band of trees, and there's our great-grandmother's house. It's a sort of run-down, small, wood-frame farmhouse. It has a porch with sagging steps, most of the whitish paint is worn off to show weathered gray boards. There's a beaten-up barn to one side, and a little wood hut just farther on. Neither one of these looks like they've ever been painted. Just the house. It looks like one of those pictures they have in history books chronicling the Depression era. One of the sad-sack houses people used to live in, right down to the scraps of faded laundry fluttering on the clothesline.

Mom pulls up to a stop in front of the house, the tires spitting out gravel and dirt. She turns off the engine. Suddenly everything is quiet and amplified all at the same time. Like the house, the car, and us inside, we're all waiting and holding our breath for what comes next.

I hear a rooster crow, and then another, a little louder than the first, like he's telling the first chicken to shut up. The roosters are a hopeful sign. Her chickens are obviously alive and crowing, haven't starved to death. So that's good. Our great-grandmother must be alive too, unless of course she croaked in the last day or two.

Mom doesn't stay in the car. Now that she's here, other than the thin sheen of sweat on her face, she's acting all casual. She gets out and gives a little stretch, a pretend yawn, glances around with a careful, disinterested look on her face. Like she's flipping pictures in a photo album and has no relation to this particular photo.

"Come on, kids," Mom says, clapping the fingers of one hand to the palm of the other twice. A sharp, brisk move-along movement. We get out of the car more gingerly than Mom, but we follow her lead and try to act no-big-deal too. Like Mom hasn't just told us she lied. That we didn't just get yanked out of school and drive all this way, and for what? Why did we drive all this way? What else is Mom lying about?

Mom marches up the steps and knocks on the door. A big blackfly tries to land on her and she shooes it away. We wait, but there is no answer. "Deaf old bat," Mom mutters under her breath. Which, if you ask me, is not a very polite way to talk of your grandmother. We never would have said those things about Nonnie to her face, or behind her back.

Mom knocks again. Harder this time, her eyebrows pulling together to meet in a storm cloud over her nose. Still no answer. "Damn! Where is she?" Mom kicks the door, which is a pretty childish gesture. I mean, the door's not responsible for her gran being gone. Mom should have called first and told her we were coming.

Mom goes back to the top of the porch steps and looks out the way we came, then turns and looks out across the field, her hand shading her eyes. Nothing. She does that thing she does with her mouth when she's thinking hard, twists her lips kind of up and sideways. "Well," she says. She goes over to the door, turns the handle, and gives the door a push. It swings open. "Of course," Mom snorts. The inside lights aren't on, and with the bright sun out here, the hall looks like a dark tunnel with bumpy, shadowy shapes.

"Are we going in, Mom?" asks Tessa. A perfectly reasonable question. Mom's opened the door, but none of us are moving. We're just standing here stuck on the porch like we're playing freeze tag and our team's lost. A weird expression crosses Mom's face. It's like there's a bad odor pouring from the house that only she can smell.

"Of course. Of course, we're going in. No sense hanging out here in the middle of nowhere. Might as well make ourselves comfortable." Mom takes a deep breath and then strides inside with the sort of determination you see on the faces of the Olympic athletes on TV right before they compete.

We sit in the living room. All lined up and well behaved, hands on our knees.

Time passes. Finally, there is a noise from the back of the house. A door opening, a screen door slamming, the shuffle of feet, the thump of something heavy being put down. An old person muttering. Mom looks like she's wrestling between running and staying put.

Staying put wins out. Mom smoothes back her hair with both hands and plasters a big smile on her face, "Gran!" she calls out, standing up. "It's me, Fran, come for a visit!" She goes to the doorway, pokes her head out into the hall. I can't hear anything from the back of the house. It's gone dead quiet. "Gran? Did you hear me?" Mom yells a little louder. "It's me, Fran, I've got my kids, brought them all the way from Newfoundland to meet you."

"Fran?"

"Yeah, Gran, it's me. Come say hello to your great-grandkids." Mom's voice is all perky, so I think she's happy, but then her head reappears with a fierce "straighten up" expression.

We sit up tall and pin smiles on our faces, but apparently she wants us to stand up because she makes a circular up, up movement with her hand. We stand in line with our hands behind our backs, faces forward, military precision. And just in time, because our great-gran appears in the doorway.

She walks right past Mom, no hug, nothing. Barely looks at her, too busy glaring at us over the top of her glasses. Nothing Nonnie-like about her. No hugs and kisses. No soft bosom or cuddly lap to nestle into. And I can't say for certain, but I'm pretty sure there's no Scotch mints tucked in her pocket as special I-love-you treats.

Our great-grandmother is old. Super old. All dried-out sinew and tendons. She looks like ancient beef jerky wrapped around a skeleton. I'm surprised her bones don't clatter as she stalks across the room toward us.

"So, Fran," she says, her voice all bitter and sarcastic. "You've finally decided to *share* my great-grandchildren with me? How kind. And to what do I owe this honor? Bob finally leave you?"

Mom's face turns two shades of red. "God, Gran. No, he didn't leave me."

"Well," our great-grandmother drawls, looking around the living room. "Where is he then? Don't tell me, he's in the bathroom?" She marches over to the doorway and shoots her scrawny neck out into the hall. "Bob!" she hollers. "Get your pahtookey in here with your family! I've got something to say!" She yanks her head back into the living room, her hand cocked around her large, dried orange-rind ear. "What's that?" Eyes glittering. "I don't hear nothing? Do you hear anything? Bob!" She slaps the living-room door hard with her open palm and sends it crashing into the wall. "Bob!" she yells, gnarled hand still pretending to be a megaphone.

Mom doesn't say anything, just stands there stuck, white-faced, at the door. We stand there too.

Mom's gran turns both palms up to the ceiling, like she's testing for rain. "No Bob," she says. "I don't see him. I don't hear him. Is he here?"

"No," Mom's voice, barely a whisper. "No, he's not."

"I knew it!" She whirls around to face Mom, surprisingly agile for such an old lady. I can't see her face anymore, but her voice is triumphant. "I told you he was a good-for-nothing bum! But would you listen? No, of course not. Wouldn't listen to your own grandparents. Well, now your grandpa's gone, died of a broken heart. And you know who broke it? You want to know?" Her face stuck up in Mom's, her bony finger jabbing into Mom's chest. "You, missy! You're the one who broke your grandpa's heart, running off like you did. Never a card or a letter. Not knowing if you were alive or dead. After all we did for you! Taking you in, raising you, even though we could ill afford it. Even though you were a spoiled little ingrate. We took you in the beloved memory of your sainted mother, God rest her soul. And how did you repay charity and kindness? By running away. Ripping up good sheets and tying them to the bed. Climbing out the window like we were ogres! You could have come and talked to us, told us your plans."

"I tried," Mom says weakly.

"Fiddlesticks!" Mom's gran cuts her off. "Do you know the gossip we had to endure? The sleepless nights, lying awake, not knowing how you were doing? If you were lying beaten and bloody, abandoned in some ditch!"

"I . . . I wrote," Mom gets out.

"Twice!" her gran shouts. "Twice in almost fourteen years! And both times to ask for money. Now you drop in, out of the blue, with your three kids that you didn't even bother to inform me you had. *My* great-grandchildren, and you couldn't be *bothered* to let me and your grandpa know? How . . . could you, Fran?" I can't tell what's going on, because her voice is raging, but it sounds like she's crying too. "And now . . . you show up . . . all sweetness and smiles . . . and expect everything to be okay? Well, it isn't . . . Get out."

"What?"

"Get out! Get out of my house!" She flicks at the air in front of Mom with her hands.

"But, Gran –"

"Don't try to argue with me, Fran. You ran off with that good-for-nothing louse against our wishes. And now he's left you. Taken up with some other hussy. Well, boo-hoo!" She wiggles her bony butt. "You made your bed, you lie in it!"

"He didn't –"

"You tell yourself whatever you need to, Fran. Just get out of my house!" The old bitch is standing now where I can see her face, and it is mean, mean, mean. Arm outstretched, skeletal finger pointing down the hall at the front door. "And take your kids with you!" I hate this old bitch so much I could spit, right there on her floor. But Mom has no backbone, she just turns around like a sleepwalker and starts to go.

"Come on!" I say, grabbing Tessa and Simon's hands and hauling them toward the door. "Let's get out of this stinky place!" And when we get to where the old bitch is standing, I don't care how old she is, I want to kick her hard right on the bony shins. But I don't, my dad wouldn't approve. I just look down at her short, rickety body like she's dirt. "I wish," I say succinctly, "that we never met you. And what's more, our dad was a good man. The best! Not that it's any of your business, but I won't let you talk crap about my dad. He didn't *leave* us, he *died*, you mean old bitch!" With that, I yank my little brother and sister through the living-room doorway and down the hall. I'm so mad my whole body is shaking, but I feel all right too. Because I saw how good I hurt her. The look I left on her face was way better than a strong, swift kick to the shins.

● ● ● ●

We're staying overnight. I don't know why. If I was Mom, I would have told the old lady where to shove her offer of dinner and a bed. Stupid old gorgon! But no, she comes hobbling out onto the porch hanging on to the rail, saying, "Fran, I didn't know. I had no idea. Forgive me. Please, come on back in and talk, okay?"

"Don't, Mom!" I said. "Let's go. *Forget* her!" But Mom didn't listen to me. She went back up those stairs and left us kids hanging around outside by the car. Well, at least Tessa and Simon were. I got in the car and strapped myself in, all ready to go, even though my butt was none too happy to be sitting in that front seat again.

Mom and her gran were in the house for a long time. Finally, Mom came back outside, looking round-shouldered and tired.

"Bring your stuff inside, kids," she said. "We're going to stay for a while." She flipped the car trunk open so Tessa and Simon could start unloading their stuff, but I didn't budge. I stayed in that car, strapped in, face set. No way I was going in that woman's house! You don't just criticize my dad and get away with it. Stupid bitch.

I stayed in the car for a long time, until my butt couldn't take it anymore and I needed to go to the bathroom. Then I had no choice. I got out, all stiff-legged, and made my way up the front steps. I found the bathroom in the hall under the stairs. I could hear everybody in the kitchen. They were eating what smelled like a very good chicken dinner, all cooked up with spice. I hadn't had chicken dinner in a long, long time, but there was no way I was going to be bought cheap like that. Did my business, flushed, washed, and went back outside. I let the door bang loudly behind me, so they'd know I knew they were eating chicken dinner with that nasty old bitch who said those mean things about our dad, and I hoped they'd feel guilty, because me and my dad didn't approve.

I didn't get back in the car right away. My body was just too cramped up. I stood by the car, though, so if anybody looked out the window, they would know my vote.

Anyway, here I am, lying in the backseat now, and it's not bad. I wrapped up the seatbelt clasps with my socks so they wouldn't dig into my side too much. I can stretch out my back and shoulders way more than I could when I was sitting upright in the front. It's quiet, though. I've got used to the sound of everyone breathing and mumbling, moving around in their sleep. But they're all inside now. Probably sleeping in beds, their bellies full of food.

I'm hungry. I should have peed outside, then I wouldn't have the smell of that chicken in my nose. I'm glad I didn't eat it, though. The old bitch probably put poison in it. I can't believe Mom went back in there!

● ● ● ●

Our great-grandmother has put all three of us in the upstairs bedroom that used to be Mom's. There's no privacy, that's for sure. I didn't know it was Mom's old room at first. Gran didn't mention it and Mom neither, but I found out.

I was playing matchbox derby races with Simon. It's not that I like playing with toy cars, but Simon was hiding in the closet crying about Dad and I wanted to cheer him up, so I offered to play. The blue matchbox Corvette that he loaned me skidded off under the bed and that's where I found the old cardboard box and dragged it out. There was a lot of dust under that bed. By the time I scooted back out, I was covered in the stuff.

Simon and I opened the box and it was like a treasure trove from the past. It was full of all kinds of things from when Mom was a kid. Report cards, a poster of Madonna wearing her boy-toy belt, a bunch of school yearbooks, a white silky banner with *Wheatonville Auto Shop* written in sky blue lettering, and a rhinestone crown. When I brought the banner and crown downstairs and showed them to Mom, she got a little smile on her face, like the memory was a good one. She ran her hand down the banner. "That's when I met your dad," she said. "He saw me sitting on the top of Mr. Walsh's car. The auto shop was my sponsor for the Wheatonville beauty pageant, and all of us girls were riding in the Wheatonville Days Parade. When your dad saw me, he was smitten. Found me later sitting at the top of the Ferris wheel with Sammy Muchler and he waited for us to come down and then asked me out. Right in front of Sammy." She laughed. "Boy, was Sammy steamed."

"What'd you do?" I asked.

She smiled big. "Went out with your dad, of course. Love at first sight. We eloped three weeks later and the rest" – Mom spread out her hands to include the room and us kids that were in it – "is history."

So that's how I know this room used to be Mom's. Our bedroom window was the very one Mom climbed out of on ripped-up sheets to run away with my dad. I have to say, I'm sort of surprised that Gran saved Mom's box of memories. I wouldn't have pegged Gran for the sentimental type. Seems more like she'd have had a big bonfire the day my mom took off. Maybe our great-grandpa made her keep it. He was supposed to have been nice.

Once we knew it was Mom's old room, everyone wanted to sleep in her bed, even though the church ladies had delivered two more twin beds a couple of days after we had arrived, and those church beds had way more spring. It felt kind of like if we slept in Mom's bed, we'd be closer to her somehow. We got into a bit of a fight about that bed and had to settle the argument by drawing straws. Simon won. Which is okay, because he's the youngest, so I don't mind. I would have been ticked off if Tessa had won, though, because she would have rubbed my face in it something fierce. I never would have heard the end of it.

There's a rather limp homemade curtain, a sheer pale-blue material, drawn back with a band of the same kind of fabric, held away from the window with a nail that the hand-stitched buttonholes pop over. I wonder sometimes who made these curtains: Mom or Gran? I don't ask, however, because when Mom first saw the things from the box of memories she seemed happy, but later that day, it was like everything bad that had ever happened to her came crashing down on her head. And for two days now she's sort of disappeared inside herself. She's taking long walks to God knows where, and I'm always scared that one day she's just going to keep walking and not come back.

She's not talking much, except when she's with Gran. And I wouldn't call that talking. A yelling fest would be a more accurate description. It's like the other day: the sky opened up while Mom was on another one of her walks and she came back soaking wet and said something about the rain, and Gran took offense. "What do you mean, 'another rainy day'? You should be damned grateful for the rain. And get yourself a towel, girl, you're dripping on my floor."

"Oh *Jesus*, Gran," said Mom, not budging an inch, rain-water making a puddle on Gran's freshly mopped floor. "Am I not allowed to speak now, *even* about the weather? Is that it?"

"You will *not* use the Good Lord's name in vain in *my* house! You watch your tongue, you do as I say, or you get out. My house, my rules!" And this wasn't a one-time occurrence. Gran and Mom are getting into screaming matches twenty-four/seven. After they finish, it's like they're all worn out, don't have any interest in discussing the old days. No. What I want to know about the past I'll just have to figure out by myself.

So even though there's nothing fancy about the room and we're packed in here like sardines, it's better than living in a car. I guess the best thing about this room is that it was Mom's and now it's ours. It's a connection to her, which is good, because

Mom seems like she's sleepwalking. Her body and her words are making the mother noises, but it's not reaching her face or her eyes. It's like it's too foggy for her to see us kids clearly. The only thing on her radar is Gran, and Gran's like the red cape they wave in front of the wounded bull.

When I walk around the room on the old wood floor, being careful not to slide my feet because sometimes you can get some pretty fierce splinters, I feel close to Mom. I think about the fact that my feet are walking where her feet walked when she was my age. Only I'm the luckier one, because I've only lost my dad, and she lost both of her parents and didn't have any brothers or sisters either. It must have been horrible for her.

Another good thing about this room is that it has its own bathroom, so I don't have to sit my butt where Gran's stinky one has been resting. Even if I'm standing right next to the downstairs bathroom and I have to go, I'd rather run through the house and up the stairs to use our toilet than the one Gran uses. That's just way too intimate for me. Our bathroom's not bad. It's small, sort of like an afterthought, but it's got everything you need: there's a tub, a sink, and a toilet squeezed in. I like the history of our lookout window. I like the fact that the ceiling's all slanted in interesting angles. The room would be pretty peaceful if Mom and Gran weren't fighting again.

"Why are Mom and Gran always so mad at each other?" Tessa asks.

"Because Gran's a bitch," I say.

"I wish they'd stop yelling," she says.

"Me too," Simon pipes in. "It hurts my ears."

"Not me," I say. "Maybe if Mom yells loud enough, Gran will kick us out and we'll get to go back home." Even though I'm pretty sure home isn't there anymore. What with all the *Immediate Attention Required* envelopes, you'd have to be pretty dim-witted not to figure out what happened.

"I am sick and tired" – Mom's voice from downstairs, rising to a shriek – "of your bullying, broomstick up-the-ass, domineering dogma! You with your high-and-mighty judgment can just go to fucking hell!"

Gran says something, but her voice is quieter and I can't quite make it out.

"Yeah . . . That would be good. I'd like to go home." Tessa sighs. "Anjulie's birthday's in three weeks and I don't want to miss it."

And I start thinking about my best friends, Emily, Morgan, and Liz, and I'm missing them too.

"I like it here," Simon says, "if Mom and Gran would just stop fighting. I like all the outdoors, running in the fields, the woods. I *love* Tom, Gran's dog. He's great!" His little cricket voice is all cheery and happy, like this is the best vacation he's ever had. "I've always wanted a dog. I like the chickens, I like Bess the cow. I like it way better here than back home."

"Well, you're dumb!" Tessa says.

"Am not!" Simon roars. "I like it! And I'm not dumb!"

"Are too!" Tessa yells, sitting up in her bed.

"Am not!" Simon bellows, doing her one better, leaping up on his bed, fists cocked.

"Shut up, you two! You're *both* dumb! Now get in bed or I'll give you what for." I screech, and that shuts them up for the most part. A few whispered "You're dumb . . ." "No, you're the dumb one . . ." But that's about it. Nice and quiet up here so we can listen to Gran and Mom fight.

"I've had it!" Mom yells. "I've had it! That's it! No more!" She's yelling, but I can tell that she's crying too.

● ● ● ●

I come down the stairs and I can feel something is different. I don't know what it is until I notice that Mom's blanket and pillow aren't all scrambled on the living-room sofa. At first I think maybe she got up early and put them away, but then when I go into the kitchen, she's not there either.

"Where's Mom?" I say to Gran, who's cooking at the stove.

"Damned if I know," Gran says.

"When's she coming back?"

"Same answer as the first," she says, dropping a large splodge of scrambled eggs on my plate. She pours herself a steaming mug of coffee and eases herself down at the table like her bones are aching. Tessa and Simon are staring at her with their pale, sleep-smeared faces.

"Mom's gone?" Tessa's fork has stopped halfway up to her mouth.

"Where'd she go?" Simon asks, looking scared.

"You better clean out your ears, young man. I just told your sister, I don't know. All these years, still hasn't grown up. Thinks of nothing, no one but herself. Sticking me here with *her* three kids. Her responsibilities, and I've got three additional mouths to feed, which, heaven knows, is not something I asked for."

"Well, I'm not hungry!" I drop my plate to the table. "So that's one less mouth for you to worry about!" I'm about to storm out, but Gran grabs me by the arm.

"Young lady!" she says. "I don't know what the rules were in your house, but in this house, we don't waste food. You sit down, and you eat that breakfast." I try to shake her off, but she's stronger than she looks. "Eat!" she barks, pointing at my plate, so I sit down and make myself eat.

"After breakfast, you kids are going to help me with the chores around here." Gran's voice sounds controlled, but I notice her hands are shaking, her coffee shivering in its mug. And I don't know if her hands have always been that way, or if this is something new today. "Since you're going to be staying, I expect you to help earn your keep. I want you to make your beds, straighten your rooms before you come down for breakfast, and no lollygagging. I don't appreciate having to wait on you all to take your own sweet time while I'm sweating over a hot stove. Simon and Tessa, I want the two of you to do the breakfast cleanup, the dishes, wipe off the table, sweep the floor. Jack, you'll do the dinner cleanup tonight."

"The *whole* kitchen?" Tessa whines, "But –"

"That's the least of it," Gran cuts her off. "You're living on a farm now, girl. Get used to it."

"We're not *living* here!" I jump in. "We're just visiting." I need to make this point clear, but Gran laughs. Not like she's amused, more like I've said something dumb.

"There are inside chores and outside chores to divide up. I'll let you kids choose. Obviously, the older you are" – she peers sternly at me over the top of her bifocals – "the more responsibility you take." Like really! I'm going to make the little kids do it all. I don't think so.

"What are the outside chores?" Tessa ventures.

"Milking the cow, mucking out her stall, feeding the chickens."

"Eww! I'll take the inside chores."

"I'll milk the cow!" Simon says, looking excited.

"You're too small, your hands aren't strong enough. Wouldn't have the strength to get all the milk out of her teats and her milk would dry up. In a couple of years, you can give it a go. Jack will milk the cow for now," she says, looking at me with challenge in her eyes. "We'll start after breakfast."

"Fine," I say. I don't know why this crazy old lady is making plans for a couple of years from now. What's she been smoking? But I'll milk that cow. And I won't show her any weakness, even if my hands do get tired. And I'll muck her stupid cow stall. What am I? Scared of a little manure? I don't think so! Gran's not going to crack me, no matter how hard she tries.

● ● ● ●

Milking cows isn't so bad. There's actually something kind of soothing about it. Getting up so early in the morning is the hardest part. Pitch-black outside, moon still bright, not even the chickens stirring, that's how early it is. I sleep with the alarm clock tucked down between the wall and my bed so the clang of it doesn't wake Simon and Tessa. Dragging my body out of sleep, out of my nice warm bed, is tough. The house and the floorboards are cold under my bare feet. Gran doesn't believe in heat, apparently. Everything is dark. I have my clothes ready in a pile by the bed so I can just step into them. Have to use a flashlight. Gran's got a solid square one that gives a nice strong light. Go downstairs, my sock feet quiet on the steps. Get my pail from by the fridge, gleaming clean from last night's washing, stuff my feet into what used to be my great-grandpa's old rubber boots, but now they're mine. It might seem strange to have my feet flopping around where his feet used to rest, but Gran's big on not wasting. I take his plaid coat from the hook on the porch and slip my arms into it. It has a faint musty smell, not a bad one. Just smells like someone else, is all. A hard-work and pipe-tobacco smell. It's weird to think about, that my great-grandpa died and I didn't even know he existed.

As I walk across the yard with my metal milk pail, the yellow-blue beam from the flashlight bobs slightly. I almost don't need it. I'm getting to know my way pretty good. I get to the barn and flip on the light.

"Hey, Bess. Good morning." The cow likes the sound of my voice. The first few days, I was kind of nervous around her. So big, and sometimes she can pin you in the corner, or by accident step on your foot and not even know it, and you've got to bang hard on her leg with your fist to make her shift and move off your toes.

But now I'm not scared.

I throw a large scoop of grain and a slab of green alfalfa in her wooden feed trough. I shovel out the stall, then let Bess come in.

Milking's hard work. Don't let anybody tell you otherwise. By the end of it, when I've finally got down to the stripping portion, my arms, hands, and wrists all feel like they're on fire,

all cramped up and about to fall off. But there's something sat-
isfying about it too. When I get into a good rhythm, and
milk's squirting out, I like the *ting* noise as it hits the pail. The
bottom gets covered with frothy, foamy warm milk, and then
when the pail gets fuller, it's not a *ting* sound of milk hitting
metal, it's a *phoost* sound of milk shooting into milk. "Phoost
. . . phoost . . . phoost . . . phoost." My face snuggling into Bess's
warm side. The contented sound of her chewing her food. The
smell of Bess and fresh milk filling the stall. It's a nice feeling.
A good way to start the day.

When we're done, I put the milk up so Bess won't accidentally knock the pail over on her way out. I untie her, give her a
slap on the butt so she knows she can go, and she backs up slo-
mo, turns herself around, and ambles out of the barn.

I don't need to use the flashlight as I leave the barn.
Morning's come. The milk weighs me down a bit, makes me
walk with my knees bent. I have to strain my body to keep
upright. I swing by the henhouse. The chickens are awake. I
can hear them jostling around the door. I unlatch the hook
and they crowd out, pecking the ground and one another, the
roosters strutting, heads thrown back, letting the world know
it's morning.

By the time I get back, Gran's in the kitchen making breakfast. Usually Tessa and Simon are down, but if they aren't I
wake them up when I go upstairs to wash and get changed for

school. That's right. School. We are going to school here for the time being. We haven't heard from Mom yet, so Gran drove us down to town last Friday, marched us into the school, and signed us up. Which was kind of a stupid thing to do, seeing as how we're going to be leaving again as soon as Mom comes back. I mean, it's sort of pointless. Us having to break in a whole new school when we aren't even going to be staying. But Gran didn't care. "Better than having you under-foot all day."

The good thing is, since this is a temporary situation, there's no pressure. I'm not even bothering to make friends. No reason to. I mean, I'm polite and all, no big deal, but I'm not going out of my way to be liked. I just ignore all the staring, curious faces. Couldn't care less what they think, if you want to know the truth.

● ● ● ●

We're doing geometry: "The study of objects, motions, and relationships in a spatial environment." Although what that has to do with all the marshmallows flying overhead is beyond me. Actually, flying marshmallows are not part of the assignment. That's just what happens whenever Mr. Holman turns back to the board. All hell breaks loose.

We're studying Euler's formula, which states that the number of faces and the number of vertices minus the number of edges equals two. We are supposed to find out if this is true of all three-dimensional objects by constructing a pyramid with a square base, using toothpicks and marshmallows. That's what we're *supposed* to be doing, although, looking around the room, I have to say I'm the only one anywhere near completion, and I've been taking my sweet time.

Nope, there's no Michael whiz kid in this class. These smart alecks aren't even thinking ahead, because once they've run out of ammunition, what are they going to build their pyramids out of?

There! Done. Considering the lack of finer building materials, my construction looks pretty decent. Eighteen minutes till lunch. My stomach's growling. That's one thing I'll say for Gran, I don't think much of her personally, but her cooking is damned good. She could make mud tasty. I don't know how she does it, but I've got some gingersnaps in my lunch right now that are begging to be eaten.

It's noisy outside. The younger grades are on lunch break, running, screaming, playing jump rope, having mud fights. God, look at that one kid, he's a walking mud ball. He doesn't seem to have anybody on his team, though; all the other boys are just pelting him with the muck. He should fight back, give as good as he gets. Oh, they're chasing him now, poor kid. Wonder where the monitor is. They're running this way, somebody should help him, he doesn't look like he is . . . Oh my God! It's Simon! Those *fuckers*!

I shoot to my feet. "Excuse me. Excuse me." The teacher's bent over some girl in an ugly shirt. I tap him on the shoulder. "Can I be excused? I need to be excused, Mr. Holman."

"Why?" He doesn't even look up at me.

"I need . . . I need to use the bathroom!"

"It can't wait? There's" – he glances up at the clock – "fourteen minutes before the bell."

"No, it can't wait. It's an emergency. I've finished my pyramid. It's over there on my desk." My insides are hopping and my heart banging in my throat, but I keep my eyes straight forward, on Mr. Holman. I don't look out the window, just in case he figures out what I'm about.

Mr. Holman sighs. "All right then. Off you go." And I'm gone like a rocket, down the hall, out the double doors, onto the playground, even though I'm not allowed. It doesn't take me long to find Simon. They've got him pinned, face down in the mud, boys holding his arms, sitting on his legs. The biggest guy is yanking Simon's head back by his hair, forcing Simon to eat a big fistful of mud. "Eat it!" he's saying. "Eat it! Say 'Yum, it tastes . . .'" And that's the last thing the little asshole gets out of his mouth before my fist makes contact. I knock that kid clear off his feet. He lands on his ass, looking shocked, holding his nose, blood streaming out from under his fingers. He starts boo-hooing. I would take the time to enjoy the sight, but I've got work to do. I dive into the pack, give those creeps a taste of what for! Bodies flying left, right, and center, and it's a good thing the lunchtime monitor finally makes an appearance, because I'm out-of-my-mind crazy. If she hadn't shown up, grabbed me by my collar, hauled me off those brats, one of those little jerks was liable to get themselves hurt bad. Real bad!

● ● ● ●

Needless to say, this was not a stellar way of introducing myself to the principal. He is not pleased, even after I explain the situation. He gives me an angry, long lecture, a lot of "Do I make myself clear?" I have to wipe off my face when I exit his office with my three-day suspension from all that spittle that came flying from his mouth. Why can't grown-ups learn how to yell without spraying flecks of spit all over the place?

Simon is none too happy with me either. *Pissed off* would be a more accurate description. He feels he was handling it fine. I don't agree. "You were letting a gang of bullies beat up on you," I say. "Pin you down and make you eat mud. That's not what I would call a situation under control. That's not an okay way of dealing with things. Especially for a Cooper!" But Simon's angry. He won't talk to me the whole bus ride home, just sits with his arms crossed, his face slammed shut. His body turned away from me, staring fierce-eyed out the window. But when we get off the bus, I get an earful. "You shouldn't have narked to the principal! Now things are just going to get worse! They're all going to tease me, having a girl fight my battles! Why didn't you just leave me alone? I can take care of myself, Jack!" he cries angrily, tears streaming down his dirt-streaked face. "I can take care of myself!" and then he butts me hard in the stomach with his head. "I hate you!" he yells. "I hate you!" He turns and runs down the road away from our driveway, his beat-up blue back-pack slapping against his back.

I want to go after him, but I don't. I know if I do, it would only make him mad and he would run even farther.

● ● ● ●

I'm in the bathroom brushing my teeth, getting ready for bed. Simon's still giving me the silent treatment and Tessa's not talking to me either. She said I was an "embarrassment," "made a spectacle of myself." Whatever! Like I care what she thinks. Anyway, the good thing about them giving me the cold shoulder is I get the bathroom all to myself. No elbows crowding me out of the sink. I get to change into my pajamas in peace and quiet.

When I take my shirt off, I find out that one of those little fuckers that was beating on Simon broke the face of my dad's watch that was hanging around my neck. My mind starts spinning, trying to figure out who did this, because when I figure it out, that person's dead! I'm not joking, I mean it. Dead. This is my dad's watch, not some Barbie doll from Wal-Mart.

I've got to focus. Okay, right after I knocked the main bully off of Simon and dove into the pack, somebody slugged me in the chest. I didn't pay attention at the time, as arms and legs were flying all over the place. But I remember quite clearly, that one fist landing. I remember thinking, "That's a dumb place to punch, the middle of my chest, all protected with bone." But that's what must have done it. I remember the fist, now all I have to do is figure out whose face was behind it. I'm still thinking about this when I leave the bathroom and get into my bed.

"Why are you crying, Jack?" I hear Simon say.

"I'm not crying," I say. "Shut up and go to sleep."

"Yes, you are," Simon says, coming over to my bed. "I can hear you and I see tears on your face."

"No! I'm not!"

"It's because of me, isn't it? I'm sorry I got so mad at you," he says, trying to pat me on the back, but I shrug him off.

"Leave her alone," Tessa says. "She's just being a stupid drama queen. Her behavior today was a disgrace. Oh boo-hoo, nobody's talking to me."

"Shut up! It's not because of that. I couldn't care less about that. And I'm not sad, I'm mad. There's a big difference."

Simon climbs up onto my bed, puts his arms around me. "Is it because I headbutted you?" he says. "I'm sorry I head-butted you, Jack."

And when he says that, something in me melts and all my anger's gone, there's just sadness left. "No, Simon, honey," I say. "It's because Dad's watch got broke when I was in that fight today."

"It did?"

"Uh-huh." I open my hand and show him the watch. Tessa comes over and looks at it too.

"That's Dad's watch?" Simon says.

"Yeah, he gave it to me."

"When?" Tessa says, bending over it, taking a closer look.

"When he was leaving for Afghanistan."

"Why didn't you tell us you had Dad's watch?" Simon says, his head tipping slightly to one side so he can see me better.

"It was a secret. I was supposed to take care of it. Keep it safe . . ." and I start crying for real now, and there's nothing they can do to make me feel any better.

● ● ● ●

The church ladies are sipping tea in the living room with Gran. I'm sitting at the top of the stairs eavesdropping, which might seem like a sneaky thing to do, but they're talking about us kids and I figure I have a right to know.

"She's a hooligan, Doris," the one with the saggy knee-high nylons says. "A danger to yourself and the community at large.

She broke poor little Richie Fitcher's nose. They had to reset it in two places."

"Why'd she punch him?" I hear Gran say. I can't tell whether she's upset, her voice is kind of neutral.

"Well, that's just it," the other woman chirps. "Nobody knows. Apparently, the boys were being boys, playing on the school grounds, and the next thing they know this maniac comes flying out of nowhere –"

"She wasn't even supposed to be on the playground." Saggy knee-highs picks up the story. "Maureen, you know Maureen, she sings soprano in the choir. Well, she was the lunchtime monitor that day, and she says the older grades weren't due outside for a good fifteen minutes. Not only was this girl being violent, but she was obviously playing hooky as well! And that's what we wanted to talk to you about, Doris. You really shouldn't have them in the house. Young people today are just not what they used to be. I know you have a big heart, Doris, but you're putting yourself in danger. Social Services has many programs that can help these young children. They're not your responsibility. Not only that, you know what we think about you living out here. This house and farm and land, it's too much for one woman to handle. You should have sold it when Horace died."

"No," Gran says. "I'm not moving. It's not going to happen."

Saggy knee-highs keeps on going. "Doris, don't be so stubborn. Ted Buchanan has repeatedly offered to buy your farm. Why don't you say yes?"

"That's right, Doris. We all worry about you, out here on your own. My mother, Mabel, you know her. Well, she moved into Serenity Valley six months ago and she just loves it! She's made lots of friends. They're busy all day, what with shuffleboard, a swimming pool, get-togethers, and golf excursions. She just loves it."

"Whoop-de-doo for her. I'm not moving. First off, I'm not alone. I've got my great-grandkids –"

"Phsst," Knee-highs snorts through her nose.

"They're good kids," Gran says sternly. "And I won't have anybody saying otherwise. Is that clear?" There's a pause in the conversation, and I can just picture Gran glaring down her nose at them. "If my Jack punched that Fitcher kid in the nose, he probably deserved it. As a matter of fact, if he takes after his father at all, I'm certain he did. Now, if you ladies are quite finished?" I hear Gran get up from her chair. "I've got a dinner cooking and kids to feed."

I'd like to stay and hear more, but when they get out into the hall, they'd be able to see me sitting on the stairs. I move fast so I'm well in our bedroom before they are around the living-room doorjamb.

I listen to them as they go out on the porch. I hear Knee-highs's voice drift up through the window. "Please reconsider, Doris. We're worried about you." I go over to my bed and lie down. I reach into my shirt, wrap my hand around Dad's watch. It's got tape to hold the glass face in place, but it still works and I can feel the comforting *tick, tick* in my hand. My heart is racing. They're trying to get Gran to sell the farm. They want her to move to that retirement community, Serenity Valley. What kind of bullshit name is that? And if they get her to go, what will happen to us? We don't know where Mom is, if she's ever coming back. What if Gran sleeps on it and decides to follow their advice? We *are* a lot of work. Three more mouths to feed. What happens if Gran gets fed up and kicks us out? Do they put us in an orphanage? A foster home? Would we get to stay together? Or be split up?

Then I think about Gran's words. How she stood up for me to those church ladies. Took my side. That's something that my dad would have done. And thinking about this, I feel my ears turn red, because I'm remembering all the mean thoughts I've had and angry words I've said about Gran. I feel so small and ashamed.

● ● ● ●

We're all eating dinner and I'm being real polite. "Yes, please" and "No, thank you" and "This dinner is delicious" when the phone rings.

"Get that, Tess," Gran says. Tessa slides off her chair, acting important, because the phone never rings here. She sashays out into the hall. I'm trying to think of something else to say to let Gran know I appreciate what she does, but I've got to be careful. Otherwise Gran will know that I was eavesdropping. She'll think I'm just bullshitting her, and won't know that I'm sincere.

"Hello," says Tessa's voice from out in the hall. And then we hear her squeal, "*Mom!*" I can't see her, but I can tell from her voice that she's jumping up and down. "How are you? Where are you? When are you coming back?"

Simon's fork clatters to the table as he bolts into the hall. And I have to say, my heart leaps too.

"Lemme talk to her," Simon says. "Lemme talk to her!"

"*Wait!* I'm talking first!"

By this time I'm out in the hall and Gran's bringing up the rear, bellowing, "My heavens, you kids, will you stop that racket!" But they aren't listening. And I'm trying to get them to behave too, because I'm worried about what the church ladies said, but nothing I do is working. Simon's too excited to pay attention. He's trying to get the phone from Tessa, who's standing on her tiptoes holding the receiver high up in the air, which is really dumb because now no one is talking except Mom. And what her tinny little voice piping out of the earpiece is saying, nobody knows.

Gran steps in and takes possession of the phone. "Fran, where the hell are you?" she barks. Not exactly the best way to make Mom want to come back. "Uh-huh. Uh-huh," Gran's only grunting, but she's making even that sound suspicious. "I see . . . And what about your kids? What do you plan to do with them? I see. Uh-huh. Nice. You have it all worked out, don't you, Fran? Nice and convenient . . . for you. What about them? Have you given it any consideration how this is affecting them? Oh, stop blubbering! You don't fool me one bit! You're doing exactly what you want. Probably had the whole thing planned before you even got here." Gran snorts, "No, I will not . . . You calm yourself down and then you can talk to them. We are going to finish our dinner before the meat loaf is rendered inedible." And with that, Gran hangs up the phone. "Back in the kitchen, you lot," Gran says, shooing her hands at us like we're chickens that she's chasing back into the coop.

"What did Mom say?" I ask as we re-enter the kitchen. "Where is she? When's she coming back?" Gran doesn't answer. She just sits down and starts chewing on her food.

● ● ● ●

"Okay, this is what we have to do," I say, pacing in front of Tessa and Simon, who are sitting cross-legged on my bed. I was sitting there too but my body was too anxious and needed to move. "When Mom comes to visit, we've got to be real good. We'll get the house spic-and-span. No arguing! We want to show her that if she takes us back, she'll have an easy and peaceful life. She doesn't know how good we are at chores. How hard we can work. We've got to show her, okay?"

"Okay." Their worried faces are turned toward me.

"And Gran too. It might take a little while to win Mom over. So we've have to make it easy on Gran. No backtalk of *any* kind. If you see her picking up something heavy, grab it before she can get it. Watch her. Help her going down steps, getting the wood. She's old, we don't want her falling and breaking a bone. Pitch in, do chores."

"We already are doing a ton of –" Tess would have kept talking, but I cut her off because this is too important.

"Do more. Don't wait for Gran to ask or remind you. If you've finished one chore, see if there is something else you can do to make her life easy. We've got to make sure she keeps us here until Mom comes to her senses. Otherwise we're going to be sent to foster homes or an orphanage, and then Mom will think, 'Well, they have a home,' and we'll be screwed. Any questions?"

"Yeah," Tessa says. "Um . . . What do we do if Gran dies before Mom comes to her senses? What will we do then? Where will we go?"

"I don't know where we'd go. We don't really have that many choices. That's why we have to take good care of Gran."

"But . . ." Tessa looks scared. "She's old. Old people die.

What if we can't stop her from dying? What then? Do you think Mom would take us then?"

"I don't know, Tessa. I just don't know."

"I've got a question," Simon says, his brow furrowed, thinking hard. "Why do the church ladies want us gone so bad?"

"They think we're too much work," I say. "That Gran's too old to have all us kids running around. They think that she'd be happier at Serenity Valley."

"What's Serenity Valley?"

"It's a retirement home, Simon. With a pool and shuffle-board and golf and all kinds of fancy things. And they think Gran would like it better there." I don't tell them about the church ladies saying I was a hooligan. Ever since I heard them talking, Knee-highs's words have been playing over and over in my head. And I think it's probably best if I don't try to get revenge for Dad's watch. That just might not be worth it, given our precarious situation. I think it might be best if I let that one go. Dad would understand because us having a home is way more important than revenge.

● ● ● ●

SUMMER

Riding on the bus and it's the last day of school! We're home free! It's been touch-and-go these last few weeks. Simon's teacher has been sending notes home, but I get Simon to give them to me on the bus before we get to our stop. Mrs. Clark has been real persistent in her requests for a meeting with Simon's parents. Like that's going to happen. Dad's just going to fly down from heaven and Mom's all of a sudden coming back to Gran's and start acting like a real Mom. I don't think so.

The messages were getting more demanding. She was talking about the need for summer school if Simon was going to have "a successful transition into third grade next year." Which is a great idea but totally unrealistic. I checked it out, and the school bus doesn't run for summer school and I'm certainly not about to ask Gran to spend the extra time and gas money driving Simon in every day. Not only that, if Gran knew that Simon was close to failing second grade and that he wasn't able to read or write yet, she might just give up on us because she might think that Simon isn't working hard or something like that.

But now we're free, free, free! And it's a good feeling.

"You got a note for me, bud?" I ask Simon once he's settled in our seat.

"Yeah," he says with a gap-toothed smile because he just lost another one of his baby teeth. He digs in his blue lunch bag and gets the note out. It's got a little smear of mashed banana on it, but I don't mind. I unfold it. Read it. Yadda, yadda, same old, same old.

"What's it say?" Simon asks.

"You know, the summer school stuff and all that."

"Am I going to go?"

"No, Simon. We don't want to bother Gran. You brought your old workbooks, right?"

"Yep!" He smiles proudly. "Right in here." He thumps his backpack on his lap.

"Good boy," I say, messing his hair. "We'll do our own summer school. Don't worry. It's going to be fine. No problem."

And it will be. I'll make sure of it. I've just got to erase the pencil marks from his workbooks and then he can do the stuff all over again. He'll be ready for third grade by the time I get through with him.

• • • •

It's dry and hot here in the summer. Feels like you're standing in front of an open oven that's turned on high. It's the kind of dry heat that makes your eyes lose all their moisture and cracks your lips up good. If I was back home I'd go for a swim, but there's no ocean to be found around here, no way to get relief from the heat, other than a ride on a special Cooper-made rope swing. So it's a lucky thing I'm an expert rope-swing maker. The swing I made is no ocean, but at least when you're swinging, it creates a little breeze, a little wind in the hair. I made it last week and hung it up in the barn. It took me a while to find the perfect spot.

I would have made us a tire swing, but Gran didn't have any spare tires lying about. At first, I was a little worried, because tire swings are the kind I know how to make. That's the kind my dad taught me how to do so well. But the swing I made in the barn is good. I just made it up as I went along. Gran let me have the rope that was looped on the back wall of the grain shed. It was my great-grandpa's rope, good and thick. "It won't do him much good where he is now," Gran said. "No, you take it, but make sure you tie it on tight. I don't want you breaking your neck. The hassle and expense of the emergency ward." But when I showed her the good knots I can do, she didn't bother me anymore. Grunted, "Fine, go on then, make your swing."

So I did. And that's where I'm heading as soon as I bring in the clothes. I'm going to cool off, riding the wind on my swing.

I come out of the basement and around the side of the house to where the clothesline is. I'm going to take the wash down because some clouds are rolling in and I'm hoping it'll rain. The plants could use the water and the well's getting low.

Simon's squatted down by the side of the house. He has a stick and is digging a hole in the dirt. He doesn't have his Lego set here, but Simon's real inventive. Tom, Gran's big brown dog, is in his usual position, stretched out on the ground, a foot or two away from Simon. He follows that kid everywhere. I'm glad Gran has Tom, even though the dog's dumb as a post. Every couple of weeks, Tom comes home, his snout, his paws, the front of his chest covered in porcupine quills, and we have to spend hours with the tweezers getting them out. And they aren't just in there lightly, suspended by the tips. Those suckers are in there deep. Sometimes the quills are buried almost all the way up to the hilt. Painful, very painful, and yet, month after month, out he jaunts to get his nose full of porcupine quills again. Not to mention the skunks Tom decides to tango with. When he comes home from one of those evenings out, the stench is unbelievable. It can make you want to throw up, that's how much it stinks! When you get a nose full of skunk smell, it makes your eyes water like you're cutting a bucketful of onions. You have to take Tom out back, wash him off with tomato juice and the hose, and still he has the smell of skunk for weeks after. The tomato juice helps, but it's no cure-all, and it's not exactly easy on Gran's pocketbook.

But Simon loves Tom, so I'm glad Gran has him, even though he's a heck of a lot of work.

Tom's tail flops once, twice, on the ground, creating a tiny dust cloud when he sees me, but that's about the extent of his greeting today. He doesn't leap up, his tail wagging the back end of his body like he sometimes does. He's probably too hot. Just one or two flops of the tail, the rest of his body stretched out flat like a rug, even his head, melded into the ground, tongue out and hanging to the side, a strand of drool dangling.

"Whatcha doing, Simon?" I say, even though I can see perfectly well for myself what he's doing. I'm trying to teach him how to be more sociable. He didn't get off on the right foot at school, so now the rocks-in-their-pockets kids in his class think he's a freak. An oddball. Granted, Simon's a little unique, but there's lots of good to him. He has a heart the size of an Albertan wheatfield and would make somebody a real good friend.

But kids are mean, like a pack of rabid dogs, going for the weak, the vulnerable, ripping them down. That's what's got me ragging on Simon so hard. I'm trying to toughen him up because I'm going to be in high school next year, on the other side of town, and I'm not going to be able to look out for Simon anymore. I'm scared to death about it because things haven't got easier for Simon on the school front. They've got harder. He's not getting beat up so much because the bully boys are scared of me, but what's going to happen when I'm not there?

I'm trying to make him more normal. The reading and writing isn't going so well, but if I can just teach him how to carry on a conversation, that would be good. That's why I just asked him what he was doing. I'm giving him practice, and now I'm standing here waiting for his answer. It's kind of slow coming, though. It's always that way when he's engrossed in something. "Well?" I say.

He looks up at me, chestnut-brown curls falling in his face. I don't know where he got those curls, because Tessa and me, our hair is straight as sticks. Anyway, the curls are sweet on him. I'm letting him keep his hair that way for the summer. What does it hurt? But I'll make sure Gran gives him a haircut a week or two before school. I'll have her cut it nice and short, close to the head, so he'll look meaner. Although, I have to say, just thinking about it already has me missing those curls.

"Digging," he says. He's lost another tooth toward the front. The other grown-up tooth is already growing in.

"Whatcha digging?" I say, squatting down beside him like it's interesting.

"A hole," he says and starts scraping at the dirt again.

"What for?"

"Well, see, when those rain clouds get over here, rain's going to hit the roof and the rain on the roof runs down and into those gutters there and if you look over here," he says, pointing up to the roof with his stick. "See up there, that's where all the rain goes from the gutters out that spout, and if I've figured correctly it should land just about here," he says, poking the center of his hole with his stick. "And I figure, I can't make a big-enough hole for us to swim in. I don't have the proper tools, but the ants are probably hot too. I mean, look how hard they're working. So if I'm right, and it does rain, and I've chosen the location correctly, then this is going to make a great swimming pool for the ants," he says, waving his stick excitedly in the air like an exclamation point. Funny little kid.

"Right on," I say, shifting Gran's laundry basket to my hip to free up my hand so I can give him a friendly punch on the shoulder.

I want him to know the difference between a friendly punch and an enemy one. I'm teaching him some of the self-defense Dad taught me. But I don't want him to haul off and use one of Dad's fancy moves on someone if they're only trying to be a pal.

I've been teaching him how to punch this summer. I make him practice over and over, holding the sofa cushion in front of my belly so he can get used to hitting hard and specific. I've taught him how to get out of a headlock too. That's an important one. Boys are always putting other boys into headlocks and then, basically, you're helpless. They've got their arm around your windpipe, cutting off your air supply. But there *is* a way out of it. You've just got to know what to do. I offered to teach Tessa too, but she just sniffed and called me weird.

I make Simon practice with me every night before he goes to bed. We do it after he's brushed his teeth and before I read him his bedtime story. I have him throw a few punches, feel his own solar plexus so he remembers what he's aiming for, and then we do a few practice runs of getting out of a headlock. I hold him, my arm tight around his neck. "Grab my arm! Tuck your chin! Tuck your chin!" I say. "Slide your hips. Good! Good! Now pull out your other arm, like that. Like that, and *pow!*" I'm feeling hopeful because he's starting to get the hang of it.

"Okay, little dude," I say. I throw another friendly one-two combination at him and he blocks me pretty well. "Go to it. Make that swimming pool. I'm sure the ants are going to be happy." And then I continue with my laundry basket to get the wash off the line so I can go and have a swing.

● ● ● ●

I've taken over cleaning the henhouse for Gran. It's a lot of work. Very smelly. Definitely not my favorite job. Chicken poop is way grosser than cow poop. *Toxic* is the word that comes to mind. I've got my tools in the wheelbarrow, the sack of chicken feed, the snow shovel, the broom with half the bristles missing, and the gunnysacks.

I fling open the door and the chickens come streaming out, pushing and shoving. A few always try to fly. They rise in the air for a couple of flaps and then crash to the ground. Actually, to be more precise, they land on the heads of about a hundred chickens all surging toward the door at once. Dust clouds, indignant squawks, roosters crowing, strutting, trying to pretend they aren't being squashed along with the rest. Fighting, pecking, screeching, claws scratching, feathers ripped out, off, flying up into the air. And then, as if to balance out the violence below, the feathers dance – catching the breeze, sailing high – and like a soft exhalation gently float down.

When I set the wheelbarrow by the door of the henhouse, a few of the stupider chickens peck at the wheel, hoping it's food. Most of them are out of the house by now, squinting and blinking in the morning sun. But there are always a few, fifteen or so, who want to stay inside, cozy and warm, maybe want to sleep a little longer or take their time laying an egg, but I can't let them stay. It's too much hard work to do with chickens underfoot. I rustle them out of their nests, bag of chicken feed flung over my shoulder, because if I left it in the wheelbarrow outside, the chickens would leap up on it and rip the grain sack to shreds. There would probably be a riot because chickens are pretty stupid.

It makes me laugh when I scoot them out of their nests because they squawk something fierce and look so indignant. I pretend they're the church ladies sitting on the toilet, pants down around their ankles, taking a dump. I chase them out the door, flopping my free arm. They dodge around this way and that, but finally I get them out and shut the door.

I get rid of them all, except for Coconut Zigzag. She's my favorite. I don't chase her out because she's not being lazy, she's being a good mom. She's broody and sitting on eggs, eight of them and one duck egg that I found and put under her, because as stupid as chickens are, ducks are even stupider. Ducks lay their eggs anywhere. In the creek, on the side of the hill so the egg just rolls on down and smashes. And once, I saw one of Gran's ducks lay an egg in mid-flight. That's how stupid they are.

I tell Gran all the time what a good hen Coconut Zigzag is. What a good layer. It would break my heart if Gran killed her and sold her to one of the neighbors for dinner, because that's what Gran does for a living. That's why she has so many chickens. She sells the eggs to people for breakfast and baking and stuff. And she sells the live chicks to people who want chickens of their own. With the bigger chickens, especially if they aren't laying particularly, well . . . it's not pretty. Their heads are chopped off. Then we have to pluck them, gut them, wash them up all clean and shiny, and stick them in a plastic bag with a red twist tie to seal it up. Then it's off to the basement fridge to keep them cool until the customers come by after work to pick them up.

So, obviously, that's not a future I want for Coconut. I'm thinking of making her a red collar out of yarn from Gran's basket. That way Gran won't grab her by accident.

I give Coconut Zigzag a big handful of chicken feed. I always move slow so I won't frighten her and get her agitated. I stroke her feathers and talk to her and tell her how proud of her I am. She lets me feel her eggs. She doesn't try to peck me because she knows I am her friend. Her eggs are warm and smooth. I like to hold them against my cheek. The duck egg is bigger, but she's still keeping it warm for me, even though it probably makes her a bit lopsided. She sits on it for me because she is good and smart, not like the other chickens. And she must have laid a new egg in the night, because now there are nine.

I fill up the applesauce lid I brought down from the house last week when I realized she was broody. I fill it with nice cool water every morning when I let the chickens out and later in the day too if I remember, in case she gets thirsty and doesn't feel like walking to the pond. She drinks from it, watching me out of the corner of her eye. Bobs her head down, gets some water in her beak, and then tips her head up and back like she's gargling mouthwash.

Now that she's taken care of, I go outside and shut the door behind me to give Coconut Zigzag a few moments of privacy. I stride out into the middle of the back field, making my loud clucking noise. When I make the clucking sound the female chickens make when they are proud and have laid an egg, all the chickens come running and I fling great arcs of chicken feed. I fling it far and in many directions so there will be food for all of them and they won't fight. I throw it far so even the shy, small, weak ones are able to eat.

Then I put the feed in the storage shed and go shovel out the henhouse. It's very hard work. I don't know how Gran did it on her own, because it's quite difficult for me and I'm young and strong. Not to mention all the work of the cow, the vegetable garden, the cooking and cleaning, doing all the laundry. I don't know how she managed.

It takes a couple of hours to shovel out that henhouse, which has to be done once a week. My shoulders and neck and back are trembling by the time I finish. And even though I work steady, I can't stay in the henhouse for too long. I'd probably asphyxiate from the fumes, so every once in a while I have to go outside for a short break and fresh air. It really stinks in there. Especially once I start lifting up the layers of poop with the shovel. Then it's like when Gran's old dog Tom cuts loose with one of his toxic killer farts. If you multiply that by a hundred-thousand-million potency, that's how bad old chicken poop smells.

When I finish shoveling, I sweep all the remaining poop and old hay out of the door. I sweep it hard so the stuff will fly far outside and not clog up the doorway. Some of the dumber chickens come running and try to peck at it, hoping it's food.

When the sweeping's finished, I pick up the gunnysacks and head off to the barn to get fresh hay.

Getting the hay is my favorite. The barn is dark and cool after all that hard work, and the air feels good on my damp skin. The shade, the smell of sweet alfalfa and hay and grains for our cow is a balm for my traumatized nose. Dust dances in the streaks of sunlight that push through the occasional slat that's gone ajar, finding its way through knotholes. Tiny tunnels of fairy light. I sometimes feel like if I put my eye up to the holes, I'd see another world, a magical one, like Narnia or something like that.

Once, a couple of months ago, I got this crazy idea, from the way the light was shining through, that if I looked out this one particular knothole, I'd be looking into heaven, and I'd be able to see my dad smiling at me. I know I'm too old to believe in that kind of stuff and I don't really, but I figured, it didn't hurt to try. So I walked over, tried not to move too fast, too eager. I mean, I knew it wasn't real, I just wanted to find out for sure. And as I expected, I didn't see him. All I saw was part of the fence and the field outside. Would have been awesome, though, if I could have seen him. I would have brought Simon and shown him, and maybe they could have talked, because I think Simon could use Dad right now.

So even though it's not really magic, it's beautiful in the barn when it's silent like it is now. Everyone's gone, nobody swinging, acting crazy and loud.

I hear a slight *ttrrrr* noise. A movement, a rustle, and I look up, overhead, and I see that there's an owl in here today. It wasn't here last week. Or maybe it's been here for a long time and I just didn't notice, because its feathers blend with the wood so well. The owl is sitting up in the rafters in the far right top corner of the barn. I climb up to the hayloft with quiet, careful footsteps and gently lower myself on the hay. I watch the owl and it watches me, sitting motionless, its slow, solemn eyes fixed on me. And I talk to the owl soft, like I talk to my chicken, and she rotates her head. I like how her head moves, swiveling like an automated toy. Like a fancier version of R2-D2 in those old-time *Star Wars* movies.

I'll bring Simon down later today and show him the owl. He'll like her. He likes all things to do with nature. He's gentle, wouldn't throw rocks or be too rowdy. He's not that kind of boy.

I stay still and send good thoughts. After a while, the owl knows that I'm not going to cause her any harm. Maybe she has babies up there too, or eggs she's hatching, because she doesn't fly away. Just stays where she is, even when I turn and look directly at her. She just stays there, fluffing up her feathers, tucked in her corner, keeping an eye on me. Reminds me of Coconut Zigzag sitting on her eggs.

Anyway, now that the owl knows me, I get up slow and start to stuff the gunnysacks with hay. The hay smells good after all that chicken poop, like summer and dust, hide and seek, friends (if I had them), and kick the can.

I take my time. I gather hay like I am collecting prayers. It feels holy somehow, reverent, because it's going to go into the henhouse and make it nice and sweet-smelling for them. I fill the gunnysacks like I'm the miller's daughter and it's precious because I've spun this hay into gold. I fill them to bursting with the beautiful, sun-dried hay, burying my face in it, breathing in the scent, the taste, the color. I'm glad nobody is here, because I know it looks crazy, but I can't help myself, it feels like church, today in this barn. The way church ought to be, not the way it is.

Then, when I am done, and all my sacks are full, I lie on my back in a deep, soft bed of hay and I sing. Nobody can hear me. They went off to town, Gran, Simon, and Tessa, to get groceries, maybe even a treat. Ice cream or a piece of candy maybe, but I don't care. I'm here in this barn, and it's glorious.

I start singing. Don't know why, I just do. Softly at first, so I won't scare the owl, but she doesn't seem to mind. Just tips her head at me, ruffles up her feathers, and then settles down to listen. So I sing a little louder, so she won't·have to strain her tufted ears to hear my songs. And she likes it, I can tell, because she closes her eyes. I sing louder and braver, until finally my voice is soaring up to the rafters, to the barn owl and her babies, and beyond.

Even though I've been told my voice isn't too good, it doesn't matter, here in this barn. I sing all the songs that I know. Radio songs, lullabies, even church songs are okay here, in this barn. I sing loud. I sing clear. Heart pounding, all this joy bursting out, filling up the barn, all of Gran's land, the whole world with my songs.

● ● ● ●

I'm washing the dinner dishes, Tessa's drying, and Simon's putting away. We've got this whole dishes thing down like a fantastic automated human machine. Sometimes we pretend to be robots, talking in robot voices, moving jerky, but not today. Gran's sitting at the kitchen table dealing with the bills and that's always a stressful time of the month. Gran gets pretty grouchy around bill-paying time, and I find I'm always holding my breath. I wonder sometimes, thinking back on all those *Immediate Attention Required* envelopes Mom was getting in St. John's, if that was the reason she decided to pack it in with us kids. We were too expensive.

I think maybe Tessa is worrying about the same thing, because she's being pretty quiet now too. Her eyes are constantly going over to Gran at the table with the bills. I worry about my sister, because she's changed a lot in the last little while. She isn't the old Tessa, all full of herself. And as much as the old Tessa irritated the hell out of me, this tamped-down, shadow-eyed Tessa is worse. Simon? Well, that's another story. Now that it's summer and he doesn't have to go to school, he's full of beans and fun. Simon probably doesn't even realize that Gran's doing the monthly bill paying. He's still being a "spic-and-span cleanup man."

"I-will-take-these-plates-to-the-cupboard," Simon says in his robot voice.

"Simon, honey, I think that's too many plates," I say in a quiet voice, hoping he will talk quieter too.

"No!" he says in an even louder voice. "I-am-a-powerful-spic-and-span-cleanup-man! I-can-carry-the-whole-world-if-I-have-to!"

"Okay, Simon," I say, whispering now. "Okay, fine. You got a good grip?"

"Yes-I-do."

He starts toward the cupboard with the stack of plates in his arms, his tongue peeking out of the side of his mouth. I feel it happen before it does. My arms go out to catch him, but it's too late. His right foot steps on the floppy toe of his left sock and he goes tumbling. The plates go flying out of his arms and crash to the floor, smashing into a million pieces. His mouth and eyes are three frightened, round O's.

Gran's sticking a check in an envelope and licking it shut

when the plates hit the floor and she levitates a good foot off her chair.

I start laughing. I don't know why. It's not funny at all, but the expression on Gran's face sets me off. Simon's bawling. Tessa's jumping up and down, hugging herself as if a werewolf just sailed in through the window.

"What are you laughing at?" Gran demands, pushing back her chair so hard it falls to the floor. "This is no joke, girl! These dishes . . . cost money."

"I know, I know," I say, but I can't stop laughing because I'm so scared.

We get sent to bed. Gran won't even let us clean up the mess. "No! *No!*" she yells, whacking the back of my legs with her broom. "Out! I want you damned kids *out* of my sight! And sweet mother of Jesus, Simon, you stop that ruckus or I'll stop it for you!" We get out of the kitchen quick. Go to bed, even though we've still got an hour and forty-five minutes until bedtime. We lie on our beds, too hot and sticky to sleep under the covers. Sunlight is blasting through the window. It won't be dark for hours. We lie silent, listening to Gran banging around in the kitchen, muttering angry words about us kids and what trouble we are.

● ● ● ●

I wake up with a start, but it's only Simon standing by my bed, tapping my shoulder.

"Why did Daddy die?"

"Wh . . . what?" I say, because it's the middle of the night and I'm not quite awake yet.

"Who did it?"

"Did what?"

"Killed our dad?"

"Our dad? Ah . . ." I try to sit up, rub the fog from my eyes. "It was . . . uh . . . an American soldier, honey . . ."

"Why? Aren't they supposed to be on the same side? Did the soldier hate him? Was the soldier a bad guy?" And I want to say, "Yes, he was a bad guy!" And if it was anyone else I was talking to, I'd follow the bad-guy comment with, "The guy was an asshole! He killed our dad!" But I can't, because this is Simon, my little brother. I have to tell the truth.

"No," I say. "It was an accident. He didn't mean to. The soldier was probably very sad when he found out that he shot our dad."

"Then why did he shoot him?"

"He thought he was someone else."

"But even if our dad was someone else, that someone else would have family too. And then his family would be as sad as our family is. So why do they have any shooting at all?"

"I don't know, Simon," I say. I wish there was more I could tell him that would help him make sense of it all, but I don't understand it myself. I'm hoping he'll go back to bed.

"Is Mom mad at us?"

"No . . . I don't think so," I say.

"Well, why'd she leave us here then? How come she doesn't come see us? Is she mad at us about Daddy?" I can see Tessa is awake now too, sitting up in her bed. I can't see her very well, but I can feel how intently her ears are turned on. I wish I had some kind of wise words to give them comfort. But I don't.

"Go to sleep," I say. "Maybe Mom will come to visit us soon. We don't know."

"What about Gran?" Tessa says. "She was really mad. Do you think she's . . . um . . . going to send us away?"

I say, "No, of course not," with more confidence than I feel, because I really don't know what Gran's going to do. I've never seen her this mad before.

"But what if she does? Then what?"

"I don't *know!*" I say, and my voice is a little sharper than I want it to be. They both start crying, and I wish I could say, "Hey, guys, it's okay! Everything's going to be all right, you guys don't have to cry." But I can't. Everything's not okay. Everything sucks, and if we wanted to curl up and bawl for the rest of our lives, I think we would damned well be entitled.

● ● ● ●

When I wake up, it's morning. Simon and Tessa are sleeping peacefully and somehow things don't seem as bad. We've got a roof over our heads. That's good. We have food. We have one another. And then, when I'm out in the barn milking Bess, I get the best idea in the whole world. I'm going to see if Gran will let me take Simon fishing. That would cheer him up. He's never been fishing before. Dad took me once, but never Simon. And it's a beautiful day. With clear blue nothing-bad's-going-to-happen-today skies. An excellent day for fishing, and last week Gran did mention a fishpond that's out here somewhere. I just have to get permission, directions, and we're good to go.

I get all my chores done fast. I feed the chickens, collect the eggs. Back in the kitchen, I help Tessa and Simon with the breakfast cleanup. I tell them about my plan and watch their faces brighten up. I was kind of surprised that Tessa wanted to come too. I wouldn't have thought fishing would have appealed to her.

We all work hard and finish the chores in no time flat. We do an extra good job to show Gran we're sorry about the plates.

When we're done, we find her out in the garden, on her hands and knees, weeding.

"Do you need help, Gran?" I say, because even though our plan was fishing, I don't like to see her rickety old body in such an obviously uncomfortable position.

"No," she says. "You kids don't know the difference between the weeds and the vegetables." She's not being mean. It's the truth. I have no idea which is which.

"We could learn if you want," Simon says.

"Yeah," I say. "We've learned how to do lots of things. We could learn how to weed the garden too."

"Some other day," Gran says. She's kind of subdued today. Probably feels guilty over some of the things she said last night. Gran weeds a little more, then stops and squints up at us. "Don't you kids have something to do? Chores or something?"

"We finished our chores," I say. "Are you sure you don't need help?"

"No."

Simon nudges me. "Then please, Gran," I say. "Um, if you don't have anything else for us to do, we were wondering if it would be all right if we could go to that fishpond you were telling us about. It would get us out of your hair for a while."

Gran thinks it over for about half a second. "All right," she says. "But be careful. Watch out for rattlesnakes, and for heaven's sake, don't fall in because I won't be there to drag you out."

"Okay," I say. "I'll watch them. Don't worry. Thanks, Gran."

I find myself wanting to give her a hug, even though her face is looking sour, but I don't think she'd appreciate it, so I keep my arms to myself. "And this way you won't have to bother defrosting anything for dinner, Gran," I say, winking at Simon, who has dark didn't-sleep-good shadows under his eyes. "Because Simon, here, is going to bring you home a nice fresh fish." Simon keeps his face stern, but his chest swells up like a little fluffball chickadee right before it sings.

Gran gets her body in a standing position and goes back to the kitchen with us. She draws out the route for me on the back of an old paper bag and gives me some of great-grandpa's fishhooks, weights, and fishing line.

"I suppose you know what to do with this," she grunts.

"Yeah," I say. "Dad taught me."

I run upstairs and get my trusty Leatherman Super Tool 200 out from under my pillow. I've got everything on it: needle-nose pliers, regular ones, two wire cutters, one for regular wire and one for the harder stuff. I used those wire cutters big-time for fixing up the henhouse window. And my Leatherman also has a serrated knife, a saw that can cut through almost anything. It's got a metal and wood file, a nine-inch ruler, a bottle opener, a small, medium, and large screwdriver, and a few other things that I don't remember what they're for, but I'm sure they're all useful. It's a beaut. Nine solid ounces of pure stainless steel and that's a fact. And as my dad used to say, "Give me a Leatherman any day. They leave that sissy Swiss Army knife panting in the dust." I say it too, whenever I'm using it around Simon. It's part of our heritage. I want Simon to know that we Coopers use only the Leatherman, just like our dad.

My mom looked pained when Dad gave me a Leatherman for my eighth birthday. "Bob," she'd said, mouth squeezing tight. "Do you really think that is appropriate?" But it was. She was wrong. My Leatherman goes with me everywhere. You never know when you'll need it. I'd bring it to school if I could. Not to bother anybody, or to make the teachers nervous, it's just that it happens to be a very handy implement.

"Where are we going?" Simon asks, trotting at my heels. "Aren't we gonna fish there?"

"No way," I say, because he's pointed at the little pond by the henhouse. "That isn't a fish-carrying pond, Simon. It's too small and shallow. Not only that, but even if it was bigger, there's too much skunk cabbage, algae, and murky swamp slime for any fish to live there."

"Oh," he says and looks up at me like I'm king.

We take the abandoned dirt logging road that runs up through the back of Gran's property and onto the park land that borders it. We'd locked Tom in the barn, but not more than twenty minutes later, here he comes, galloping up the road after us, nose in the air, ears flopping, tongue hanging out the side of his mouth, big dog smile on his face. None of us feel like turning around and bringing him back home. It would be pointless, because that dog's like Houdini and he'd just escape again, so we let him stay. But I tell him, in no uncertain terms, that he'd better be quiet and behave.

Gran's property is pretty big. "Thirty acres," is what she said when I asked her the other night. She was sitting in her rocking chair, the wood runners against the floor creaking as the weight of her flour-sack body shifted back and forth. The dinner dishes were done. We'd sold four fryers and six dozen eggs, so it was a good day. I'd been wondering and working up to the question for a long time. I didn't want her to think I was being nosy, but then I figured, Why not? The worst she could do was make that lemon-sucking face and say, "Mind your own business, girl," or something like that.

She didn't, though. "Thirty acres," she'd said, knitting needles flying. She's making an awful-looking maroon sweater that apparently she's expecting me to wear next year. "Property rich, cash poor," Gran had said. "I own it, yes, but how long before the government takes it from me? It's getting harder and harder to scrape up the money to pay the land taxes, not to mention the expense of the three of you. Lord have mercy. It's not easy. No, it's not."

And I stopped asking her questions, because I certainly didn't want her to continue to think about how much money it was costing her to feed us. So I just said, "Wow, Gran, that sweater sure is coming along. This is great! I've never had somebody make me a sweater before."

Thirty acres. That's an enormous property, as far as I'm concerned. Hell, we only had a yard back home in St. John's, and we thought *that* was great.

The fishpond is quite a ways from the house. It takes a good hour, hour and a half, to get there. But Tessa and Simon don't complain, even though we're all hot and tired, dusty from the walk. It's nice to get off the farm and do something different for a change. My legs are all itchy from grass slashes and hives. I should have worn long pants, but it's too hot. I can tell we're almost there because I recognize the bend in the road from Gran's drawing, the downed tree lying across it.

"We're almost there," I say. "Now, you have to be quiet, you don't want to scare the fish." As I say it, I become exaggeratedly quiet in my moves and my voice. Picking up and placing my feet carefully, whispering. They follow suit, eyes shining like Christmas tree lights. Simon hugs himself with excitement. All their tiredness from the walk is gone.

We climb over the downed tree, round the bend, and there's the fishpond with its pussy willows and bulrushes. The sunlight is glistening and glittering, sending sparkles dancing off the water. The cool, cold water that beckons like a promise. I can see a mallard duck paddling on the far end, a string of brown-speckled ducklings trailing behind her.

"Can we eat first?" Tessa whispers, throwing herself on the ground. "My legs are tired, and I'm hungry." I have to say, I agree with her.

Actually, looking at that water, I'd love to say, "Hey, let's forget about fishing, guys, let's go for a swim." That fishpond is calling to my hot, sweaty body big-time. Looks good and cold.

I don't offer up this suggestion, though. I promised Gran fish for dinner, and there's no way I'm letting her down. If we went crashing into the water now, we'd most definitely scare the fish. Maybe later, after we've caught a fish or two, maybe then I'll recommend a swim.

"Look, I'll tell you what," I say. "Why don't you guys eat lunch and rest your legs while I gather us some good fishing poles?"

"Aren't you going to eat?" Simon says.

"I'll eat a sandwich on the fly," I say, like I'm hip-hop cool. "I've got to get us some primo fishing poles. Now," I say, just like my dad said to me, "the trick with a successful fishing outing all lies in the pole. The quality of it. If you just pick up some old dry stick off the ground, you're going to be disappointed. Because if you get yourself a nice, plump, juicy fish on the end of your pole and you've got yourself a bad stick? Snap! That baby's going to break at the first scrap of fight the fish puts up and bye-bye dinner. You have to get a good pole. That's the first rule of fishing." Then I grab myself an egg-salad sandwich and head off.

I have to scout a bit before I find a good tree with the right kind of branches that are straight and true. You've got to use living branches, because they still have sap flowing in them that makes them slightly supple. You don't want too supple. A wishy-washy branch will just fold up, bend in two. "It's got to have just the right amount of firmness and strength to be a good fishing rod." That's what my dad said, and he knew fishing.

I snap the branches first, twist them a bit, so there's less to cut through, then I get my miniature saw going. It doesn't take long. Maybe five minutes, seven tops, and I've got us three fine triple-A-plus fishing rods. I swagger back to Simon and Tessa and squat down by my backpack, take out the nylon fishing line, the hooks, and the three small black ball-bearing weights Gran lent me.

I make fast work of it, tying on the line, the weights, and the hooks. Then we've got to dig for worms in the soft, warm mud of the bank. We get one for each hook and a couple of spares. We stick the spares in the plastic Thermos cup with a little splash of water and a fistful of mud. Then we wrap up the cup in one of the egg-salad sandwich baggies and hope the worms don't suffocate in there.

I show Simon and Tessa how to hook the worms. Tessa is surprisingly into it. I would have thought she would have gone screaming when I had to stick the hook up the worm's butt, because I really hate this part, but Tessa's fascinated.

"Let me do it. Let me do it. I want to do my own," she says. And she does it real well, way better than me, her freckled nose scrunched up in concentration.

I tell her, Good job. Maybe a little praise will get her to worm Simon's hook. And it works, she does.

"Okay," I whisper. "We've got to spread out, can't all be fishing in the same spot."

"Why?" asks Simon, like I have all the answers.

"Well, because it would look too suspicious if all of a sudden three juicy worms just drop into the water all at the same time."

"Yeah, dummy," Tessa says. Not only is she not whispering, she's being mean too. I give her my you-want-a-punch-in-the-nose? look. That shuts her up.

"Okay?" I say.

"Okay," he says, face solemn, like there is a right way and a wrong way to do this and he hopes he doesn't screw up.

"Have fun." I give him a little steering push with my hand. "Go on now, scoot." Tessa's already on her way, picking out her spot. She's competitive that way.

We spread out. Silent fishing ninjas. Quiet as the fog. Our footsteps are so soft that even the frogs think we have gone and they start up their singing again.

I find a prime spot, up a tiny embankment, and cast my fishing line into the water, sit down in the shade. The tree's trunk is close enough to the water that I can sit and fish all at once. I lean my back up against the tree. The bark's rough pattern presses through my thin cotton shirt. It's beautiful here. Peaceful. The dragonflies are out, showing off their multi-jeweled tones, hovering, dancing, kissing the water, but just barely, a game of dare, they don't want to get waterlogged, dragged in. A trout jumps, arches, and enters the water again with a splash. And I want it. I want that trout on the end of my line. I want to be the hero of the day. "Come here, trout," I whisper, jiggling my line a little to be tempting. "I've got a nice juicy worm for you. Good and fresh." I send it you-are-hungry thoughts with my mind. I really think it's working, but then I hear a noise. My first thought is, Maybe it's a grizzly bear, attracted to the smell of our egg-salad sandwiches and the promise of fish. But it isn't. When I look up, Simon's standing nearby, his fishing pole dangling loose in his hand.

"What . . . What do I do if . . . I catch one?" he says, face pale.

"If you feel a fish nibble, you wait for a second or two and then you go like this." I demonstrate, giving my own pole a little sharp tug. "That sets the hook."

"And then what?"

"And then . . ." I was about to go into the logistics of it, how you battle the fish in, take its fighting, thrashing body off the hook and bash its head in with a double-fist-sized rock. But I can see by Simon's face that this whole scenario maybe falls under the category of "too much information." It would only stress him out. He couldn't even watch the hooking of the worm. Kept his eyes squeezed shut and his fingers stuffed in his ears. How's he going to handle killing a fish?

"And then," I say cheerfully, thinking fast. "Why then you call me, and I'll bring the fish in for you."

"You'll . . . bring it in?"

"Yes. I'll bring it in. That is, if you want me to."

"Okay," he says, looking much relieved. "Okay, I'll call you." He turns around and trots off. Simon only gets one or two steps, though, before his feet slow. "Wait," he calls out in a normal-volume voice, then jumps at the sound of it, looks around guiltily, shoulders hunching up around his neck, like a box turtle, trying to disappear. He tiptoes back. "But, Jack," he whispers, "if I call you, you won't be able to hear me, because I'm only supposed to whisper."

"Don't worry, dude," I reach out my hand, mess Simon's hair, give him a jaunty fisherman's wink. "You got a fish? You call me. Good and loud and I'll come running."

"Good and loud?"

"Good and loud."

"Okay," and off he goes again, tiptoeing softly, while Tom happily follows, totally destroying Simon's effort of subtle stealth-walking because that dog is tearing through the under-brush like a hippopotamus in heat.

I settle back into my tree and try to get my mind back on fishing. I jiggle my pole a bit. It's hot, even in the shade. Dry too. I can taste dust in my mouth. Guess that's why cowboys wear handkerchiefs across their noses and mouths, they get tired of sucking up dust. I'd wear a bandana now if I had one. I'd be the fishing bandit. Jack Cooper, catching fish to feed the poor.

Actually, we are the poor. Gran mentioned to Mona, one of her church-lady friends, the difficulties she was having getting us ready for school, and then Mona talked to a bunch of other church ladies, and they talked to Reverend Drysdale, and the whole lot of them decided to take up a collection to help Gran pay for our school supplies. Can you believe that? It was so embarrassing, sitting in church last Sunday, listening to the reverend preaching on about how "It's all well and good to donate to the earthquake victims and the war-torn countries, but what about here? What about the private, proud, and personal battles that are being fought in our own town? What about a beloved, brave member of our own church, who shall remain anonymous . . ." And at this point, half the ladies of the church turned around and smiled and nodded at Gran, who was just staring forward, her back stiff as a board. She was not nodding back. Her face flushed, as she tried to pretend she didn't know what they were nodding about. But I figured it out and wanted to die.

And that's where I am, in the church with Gran, when Tessa's ear-piercing scream brings me back to the pond with a fishing rod in my hand.

I leap to my feet, almost decapitating myself on a low branch, thinking Tessa's gone and fallen into the fishpond or something else equally dire. But, no. I round the bulrushes and see that she's got herself a fish. The first fish, wouldn't you know it. I can tell she's got one because her line's pulling hard and bucking.

"I've got a fish! I've got a fish! What do I do?" She's screaming at the top of her lungs, so you can kiss me or Simon catching a fish good-bye. I can see Simon on the far end of the pond springing to his feet, his hand flying up to his forehead to shade his eyes from the sun.

"Pull it out!" I yell, sprinting toward her.

"How?"

"Just pull! Pull on the pole!"

Sometimes Tessa takes things too literally. So she doesn't just pull that fish in. She gives her fishing pole a mighty yank and that damned fish goes catapulting out of the water, sailing up into the sky, and finally comes to rest a good fifteen or twenty feet in the air, dangling from a branch in the tree about ten feet behind her.

"Jesus Christ, Tessa!" I yell. I was going to say, Can't you do anything right? But then I see her face, it's filled with the glory and excitement of catching her very first fish, and the fear of it too. Like she's worried that fish is going to be stuck dangling from that tree forever. And she's jerking and yanking on her pole like a crazy person, but the fishing line is caught up in that tree and tangled good.

So instead of telling her she's a screwup, I say for the second time today, "Good job, you caught a fish," and then, because she starts crying, I say, "Don't worry, I'll get it down."

I kick off my running shoes and scale up the trunk of the tree. I get to the branch Tessa's fish is dangling from and start to inch my way out. Tessa's screaming, "Don't fall, Jack. Be careful, don't fall." So, I guess she loves me after all.

It's touch-and-go. The branch isn't too thick. I get halfway out to where the fish is caught up and make the mistake of looking down. It's a long way down, doesn't look very soft. Probably will break my neck if I fall. And the idea of that makes my hands slick with sweat. I want to turn back, but I'm already out here and Tessa's counting on me to get that stupid fish down. I slide along the branch on my belly, holding my breath to make me lighter. I stretch my fingers out as far as they can go and I can touch the fishing line, just barely. I'm sweating all over now, can feel it trickling on my skin like ants.

"Okay, Tessa!" I call.

I ease my Leatherman out of the front pocket of my shorts, keeping the rest of my body and my other arm wrapped tight around the branch. I manage, somehow, to pull the knife part open with my teeth, stretch my arm out, and cut the fishing line.

The fish falls like a rock, right into Tessa shirt that she's holding out in front of her like a firefighter's trampoline. She closes her shirt around her prize quick, because that fish is still jerking and she doesn't want it to flip out and make its way back to the water.

"What do I do now?" she yells. I can't answer right away. I'm too busy easing myself back to the main part of the trunk. I don't know what I was thinking, being the hero, venturing out on such a skinny branch. I wasn't thinking clearly, that's for sure. If I got hurt, who would help Gran with the chores? Who would feed the chickens, milk the cow, take care of Simon. Stupidity is what it was. Showing off, saving the day. And now that the dumb fish is safely down, my adrenalin has stopped pumping, and I honestly don't know if I'm going to make it back to the ground in one piece.

"What do I do?" Tessa yells again, her face tipped upward, glowing at me.

"Just a minute," I grunt, my Leatherman in my teeth. I'm inching backward on this damned branch. My shirt has slid up and the bark is scraping my belly big-time. My stomach is going to hurt tonight. And then I feel it. My stretched-out toes hitting the main part of the tree. I scoot back a little more, and some more, until my legs are wrapped securely around the trunk, and that's good. It's a much better position to be in, because even if the branch were to snap, I wouldn't plunge to the ground, would probably just scrape all the skin off the inside of my thighs, another good reason why I should have worn jeans. It was really dumb of me to wear shorts.

"Okay," I say to Tessa, after taking a deep lungful of thank-God-I'm-alive breath. "You've got to bash the fish on the head with a rock."

I start to make my way down the trunk of the tree, finding crevices and branches for my toes and fingers to cling on, dig into. "Make sure it's a good-sized one," I say, but glancing over my shoulder, I can see further instruction is not necessary. She's already found a rock and is swinging it down on the fish's head like there's no tomorrow.

By the time my feet are safely on the ground, Simon has arrived at the base of the tree, and the bashing in of the fish's head is done. The fish is dead, and Tessa is holding it up, beaming proudly.

We stand around admiring it. We hold its slippery body in our hands, running our fingers both ways. The smooth, sleek cutting-through-the-water way, going in the direction of the fish's scales. And the other way too, against the scales. It feels so different this way. Its skin is rough, like a cow's tongue. Tessa is talking, babbling excitedly, her words tumbling over one another like an overflowing brook. How it happened. How she felt the fish nibble. How I said pull. How she pulled, she *pulled* all right! Fits of laughter here, from all of us. "That fish went flying into the tree like a 747, and then Jack climbed up into the tree and saved my fish. I was so scared Jack was going to fall, and then what would we do? We'd have no one." Here she hugs me tight around my waist with her free arm, the fish clasped to her chest with the other. Simon comes over and hugs me too. I act all gruff, say, "Okay, okay. Enough of that mushy stuff." But they don't let go for some time, and I feel all warm and loved in my belly.

● ● ● ●

Our mom's coming for a visit today. The summer ran away with her, she said on the phone. Didn't realize how fast time had flown. A crappy excuse for abandoning your kids, but I've got to let it go. It's all water under the bridge, as Gran would say. Mom's coming, so that's good. Actually, even though she left us here, we're pretty excited about seeing her, because now we finally get to implement our secret plan. Mission X: get Mom to want us back.

I'm cleaning and scrubbing like a fiend. I can hear Tessa in the living room, pushing the old vacuum cleaner around, banging into things. That machine's on its last legs and tends to leave more dirt than it picks up. I've patched up the vacuum hose with thick black tape I found in my great-grandpa's toolbox. It seems to be helping a bit, but it's only a makeshift measure. It's just a matter of time before the vacuum cleaner bites the dust.

I'm in the kitchen, making it shine. I know it's silly. Our mom is either going to want to take us home with her or not. She either loves us or she doesn't. No amount of housework is going to change that.

I guess it's a mix of things for me. It's pride too. If Mom doesn't want us, then I want her to think we're doing just fine and dandy without her. Because I'm starting to figure out the score. If Mom wanted us, we'd be with her right now. She wouldn't have pretended we were "just coming out for a nice little visit with our great-grandmother" and then left us here, saying, "It's a temporary solution" when it's not. We've been living with Gran for four and a half months now, and there's no end in sight. So, although I'm hopeful about Mom coming to visit, I'm realistic too.

Now Tessa, she's got a different take on it. Not that I blame her. I probably would too, if I was her age and Mom's favorite. Tessa's been cleaning ever since Mom's phone call three days ago, when Mom said she was coming. Tessa wants this place perfect. She wants herself perfect, so Mom will see the light. And I understand, but it kills me to see the shy hope in Tessa's face, and Simon's too. I wish I'd never come up with Mission X, because they've got everything riding on it, and as Mom's visit draws closer and closer, I'm starting to think that maybe it's a lost cause. But I don't know what to do. They're so excited. Last night Tessa kept us up late, trying on outfits, like if she picks the right one it will make a difference. She wrapped her hair up in Gran's pink sponge curlers before she went to bed and spent the whole night tossing and turning, because those curlers are uncomfortable to sleep in. And Simon woke me up early, bouncing on my bed, saying, "Get up! Get up! Mom comes today!"

"Don't know why you're all making such a fuss," Gran snorts at the breakfast table. "Damned foolish, if you ask me!" But she's cleaning too, so hard that the sweat's running down her face. I think for Gran it's about pride too. A show-no-weakness, we're-doing-fine-thank-you kind of thing. She's on the porch now, banging the dust out of the cushions on the old flowered sofa. Next she'll sprinkle some water on the floor so when she sweeps the dust won't just fly up in the air and then settle back down again, right where it was before.

I'm scrubbing the kitchen floor when Simon bursts in. He doesn't even remove his shoes, which pisses me off, because, obviously, I am *mopping* the floor.

"Simon, young man!" I yell. "Watch my floor!" But he doesn't stop in his tracks like I'd expect. He just keeps tearing toward me, starts yanking on my arm.

"You . . . You've got to come . . . You've got to come! Come quick . . . Please, Jack. Please!" And he's blubbering like I haven't seen him do in a very long while. Crying so hard he's having trouble getting his breath and is all white around his nostrils and eyes. "Please . . . Please . . . Please!" He's pulling me, dragging me to the door. I didn't realize he was that strong. I go with him, even though Mom's due to arrive sometime in the next hour. If I was thinking straight, I wouldn't be going on an outdoor adventure with Simon. There's too much at stake. I'd be finishing up the kitchen floor. I'd be getting out of my housework clothes and into my good ones. I'd be making sure Simon looked nice and his nails were clean and his hair combed. I want Simon to look his best, so Mom will swing him up in her arms and give him a hug and a kiss. I want her to tell him what a fine boy he is. That she loves him and has missed him so much.

But here we are. Mom's due to arrive, and neither one of us is cleaned up. The kitchen floor is only half done, and we're racing through the field. Simon's pulling hard on my hand, urging me along, but I'm already going as fast as I can because I don't have my shoes on. Sharp rocks and prickly burr bristles are slowing me down.

"Where are we going, Simon? " But he's crying too hard to make any sense.

We get to the other side of the field and I can hear old Tom barking up a storm. We scramble down into the dried-up creekbed, turn the corner, and there's Tom, darting in and out, snapping at something that is under a good-sized boulder. And even though I can't see what it is, I know. I know in my belly.

"We need a stick!" I yell. "A big one!" We both tear back up the bank, eyes flipping this way and that.

"There's one!" Simon yells. Now that we're here at the scene, his voice is back and he becomes a man of action. He finds a great stick and has already started dragging it toward me by the time I reach him.

"Good! Good job!" I say. "This will work fine." I hoist the stick over my shoulder. It *is* a good one, the size of a baseball bat. I run as fast as I can, Simon close on my heels, to where Tom is going crazy, barking and snapping and gnashing his teeth. My feet don't even feel the rocks now. The only thing that matters is saving Simon's dog.

I was right. It's a rattler. A big one. A prairie rattlesnake. It looks just like the pictures. I can see the black-and-tan-and-brown pattern going down its back. I can't see its rattle, though. That part of it is under the rock. Just the upper part is exposed, coiling and springing, black eyes glittering, mouth open wide, fangs at the ready, spitting poison and hissing. It moves fast. Fast and deadly. Weaving its body, then arching up and striking out, sudden and swift. Almost gets Tom, just misses the lower part of his jowls.

"Pull him back!" I yell. "Pull him back!" I can see out of the corner of my eye that Simon is trying. He's got his arms wrapped around Tom's neck, but Simon's no match for that dog. Tom's eighty pounds to Simon's sixty-five, and Tom is a dog possessed.

So even though Simon's got his heels dug deep into the ground and is pulling back with everything he's got. Tom's bearing forward toward the snake, barking and snapping and showing his teeth, dragging my weeping brother along with him.

Keeping my eye on the rattler, I kick behind me and hit Tom hard in the chest with my foot. He yelps and retreats momentarily. I have to move fast.

The snake's head swivels, rotates around, locks on me. And I'm scared, but I don't have time, I bring my stick down hard, both hands gripping the branch tight, but I miss. Just hit dirt and a part of a rock, jarring my arms and teeth. The snake moved too fast. It lashes out again before I've got Simon's big stick back up over my head. But thank God I'm paying attention and I jump out of the way, my heart pounding, a metallic taste in my mouth, like I've been sucking on a fistful of change. Because that rattler almost bit my foot. Wish I was wearing shoes.

I bring the stick down again and catch the side of the snake's neck. I don't get its flat pie-server-shaped head, but I know I've stunned it, because even though it's already moving back under the rock, recoiling, getting ready to lash out again, it's moving a little slower. It strikes at me again. I jump to the side. And as it's swiveling its head around toward me, I bring the stick down again. Hard and accurate this time. Right on the snake's head. I feel the impact as it hits. I strike that rattler over and over and over again until its head is smashed flat into the ground.

Then there's nothing. Just the sound of the wind in the trees. My jagged breath. Simon's hiccuping sobs.

I'm shaking. I feel Tom move up beside me. He's not barking anymore. His warm, furry body leans in against my leg.

"It's done," I say to no one in particular. I'm suddenly weak-legged and wobbly.

I make myself move. Be practical. Take out my Leatherman, pin the snake's head with the stick. I cut the head off, dig a hole, and bury it. "Even though a rattler's dead," I say to a wide-eyed Simon, "it can still bite, even if it's just a skull. So if you ever kill a rattler, you've got to cut off the head and bury it, so it won't poison someone out for a walk."

I don't know how I knew this. Gran must have told me. Or maybe I overheard one of the boys bragging at school. I don't know whether it's true or not, but just in case, I take the precaution. Once the head's buried, I stamp the ground down, and Simon and I roll a big rock over the spot so Tom won't come back and dig it up later.

I feel slightly nauseous, looking at the snake's twitching, headless body.

"What are we going to do with it?" Simon asks.

"I don't know . . . What would you like to do?"

"We could bring it home. I could put the skin up on the wall over my bed. Cut off the rattle and save that too."

And I want to say, Yuck, Simon! That's gross! I don't want

a dead snakeskin on the wall, that's my bedroom too, but I catch myself just in time, and keep my mouth shut. I don't want to discourage him from being a boy. Wasn't that what this whole summer was about? Me trying to toughen him up? So I'm not about to nip that in the bud, no matter how much I don't want a dead snakeskin, especially one that I murdered, staring at me while I try to go to sleep.

"Cool," I say. "Good idea." I get a medium-sized stick, slide it under the snake. I have to shut off my stomach to do it, make myself think of newborn kittens and other cozy things. I get the snake up and balanced after a few tries, its still-twitching body draped over the stick. We make our way back up the creekbed, across the field, through the yard, and in the back door.

Mom's here. She arrived early, wouldn't you know it. She's sitting on the sofa in the living room with a mug of something in her hand. I don't know what she's drinking these days. The last time she called us she was going on about chai to Tessa. Talking about how good it is, and how much Tessa would love it. And she's right, the way Tessa's feeling right now, she'd love the taste of boogers if Mom said so. Anyway, Tessa was talking all about how Mom said we would love this great coffee house on the corner of Mom's block and they make the best chai and someday, when we're living with her, Mom's going to take us all to this fancy coffee house for a cup of this chai.

To be honest, I was sort of falling for it until Gran snorted through her nose and said, "Sure . . . and pigs will fly." Which made me laugh.

Tessa gave me a look, like she felt betrayed that I was laughing at Gran's joke. But I have to say, it was funny. Come on, we'll all go for "chai." Mom hasn't even had us visit her fabulous Calgary apartment! Not once in the four and a half months she's been there. Mom always talks about it like we were there last week, but come on, get real.

So there Mom is, sitting on Gran's sofa in her city clothes. She never used to dress like this before, when she was our mom. She used to wear jeans and sweats, or sometimes she'd put on a pretty top and would curl her hair, put on a dab of that pink shiny lipgloss she liked to wear when Dad and her would go out on the town. But she's changed. Her hair's cut short and is a different color. Some of the old brown color is still there, but it's not the same. She's got a zillion more highlights, blond streaks and tawny red-gold ones, and it's layered and blow-dried so it puffs around her face. And she's wearing makeup, not just a dash of lipgloss anymore. She's got some brown and lilac stuff on her eyelids and tons of mascara. She doesn't even look like my mom. I find myself wondering if she smells the same. For a second I want to crawl up on her lap, like I used to as a little girl. I wouldn't, God no. But I want to breathe her in deep, just for a second. I want to smell her to see if she still has that mother smell she had. I want so bad to crawl up on the sofa and have her put her arms around me . . .

"What the *hell* is *that*?" I hear Mom say. It startles me, because I really felt like I was snuggling on the sofa for a minute.

Not anymore. I'm back in the hallway. Me and Simon both. I know we look bad. Like something the cat dragged in. This is not how I imagined we would look when we finally got to see Mom again. We don't have our school clothes on. Our hair isn't brushed. I don't know about my face, but Simon's is dirt-streaked and tear-stained. Worst of all, we are carrying the bloody carcass of about four feet of snake, slung over a stick. It's dripping blood out of its headless stump onto the floor.

"Um . . . a snake," I say. At the disgusted expression on Mom's face, I find I have to explain the rest of the story, so she'll understand and won't think bad of me, but I can't seem to look up at her. I'm too embarrassed to look at anything but my feet, and even my feet shame me. They are filthy, scraped up, and cut. This is not the way I wanted Mom to see us.

To make matters worse, there's Tessa sitting beside Mom on the sofa, pressed and polished. She's wearing her party dress, which I notice, with no small satisfaction, is not looking so good. It is getting just a tad tight, like she had to stuff her little sausage body into it and at any moment the zipper in the back might give way.

But even thinking this mean thought, I know she looks a whole lot better than Simon and me, that's for sure. Sitting there with her fake curly hair and a sweet "I'm good" smile on her face. Her ankles crossed and hands tucked neatly in her lap. Typical. Mom shows up and Tessa slips right back into her old tricks of being Miss Goody Two-Shoes. Making us look bad. Because, I mean, come on, if you only had room for one of us in your city apartment, which one would you chose? I think the answer is a no-brainer. Suckhole Tessa would win, hands down.

Needless to say, my mom is none too pleased with my appearance or with the dead snake dangling from my stick. She acts like I'm a hooligan who's corrupting her baby boy. Not that she's been showing much maternal interest in him for the last little while. She isn't interested in my explanations. In that tight-lipped way of hers, she says, "Jacqueline Miriam Cooper, you throw that disgusting thing outside and get yourself upstairs in a bath with plenty of hot water and soap." Yeah, right, like I'm going to take a cold bath? "And don't come down until you are clean."

"Yes, ma'am," I say, turning to go.

"Wait, missy!"

I stop. "Yes, ma'am?"

"You take your brother with you."

"Yes, ma'am," I say, Simon tucking his little hand into mine. We go out back and lay our snake on a rock, for later. I'm not throwing it out. She's not the boss of me. Besides, I told Simon I'd keep the skin and rattle for him and I don't intend to break my promise.

Some great homecoming.

I clean up Simon first. I run him a bath and help him wash his hair, because he still sometimes gets soap in his eyes. While he's rinsing, I lay out his clothes. A good outfit, clean jeans, a shirt that fits and doesn't have any stains. I get him fresh socks, ones with no holes, and comb his hair.

"Mom's mad," he says, looking worried.

"Nah," I say. "She's mad at me, not you."

"Why?"

"Ach," I say, tougher than I feel. "Who knows? Who cares?" I give his head a pat. "Go on," I say. "Go down and see her."

When he leaves the room, I shut the door behind him and sit down on my bed.

I'm going to get washed up, I just need a moment or two, is all. But then I hear Gran's footsteps coming upstairs. I don't know what to do. I don't want her to see me all vulnurable like this, so I scramble into bed, my dirty snake-killing clothes still on. I pull the covers up over my head, face my body toward the wall, just in case. I squeeze my eyes shut and pretend to be asleep. I hear the door open. I hear Gran walk over. I know it's her. I can tell by her tired footsteps and how she favors the right leg, puts more weight on the left.

"Jack," Gran says. I don't answer, keep my eyes shut like I'm asleep.

"Jack, honey," her voice is softer, gentler than normal. She puts her hand on my shoulder. I can feel it rest there through my blanket. "I'm proud of you, girl," Gran says. "Simon told me what happened. What you did took a lot of bravery. Don't let anyone tell you otherwise."

She's there for a moment longer, then she straightens up and leaves. A good thing too, because when she rests her hand on my shoulder and says I did good, my eyes fill up. I don't know why. Disappointment, I guess, because we'd been planning Mission X for such a long time and now I'd shot it all to hell. A damned stupid reaction, but that's what happens, and by the time the bedroom door shuts behind her, not just my eyes, but my whole body is crying hard.

Finally, I calm down and am able to take my bath, wash my hair, and get dressed. I don't put on my school clothes, even though I had them laid out. It seems like a waste of time. I'm already in the doghouse with Mom. So why bother? She's not worth it.

I don't wear my worst, but I don't wear my best either. I wear my in-between clothes: cutoffs and a clean top. I comb my hair and come downstairs.

I don't go into the living room where Mom is holding court either. I go into the kitchen to finish up the floor, but when I get there, I can see it's done already. Sparkling clean, all my supplies put away.

Gran is at the stove, cooking up a storm.

"What are you making, Gran?" I say. I don't look her in the face because I'm still feeling shy about what happened before. Her kindness. I don't want her to think she's going to have to be soft all the time with me now. And I'm not just making polite conversation, what she's cooking smells really good.

Damned if Gran doesn't say, "I'm cooking up that snake you killed." Like she's talking about the color of the sky. "I'm cooking up that snake you killed," normal as can be, shaking a little more pepper into the pan.

At first I think maybe she's kidding with me because she knows I was sad. But when I look at her, her face doesn't seem like she's joking. So I sneak a peek into her pan and there it is. I wouldn't know what it was if she hadn't told me, but now that she has, what she's got sizzling in that pan is clear as day. She's obviously skinned and cleaned it. Cut it in one-inch cubes and is frying it up with a little margarine, some minced onion, salt and pepper, and a handful of flour. Smells okay, but I have to say, I'm not planning on eating it. No way, no how. I don't eat snake.

"What are you standing there staring for?" Gran says, lifting the lid of her pot, steam billowing out as she gives the rice a stir. "Set the table, child," and I do. Slow and steady, wondering what's going to happen next.

I cut a couple of peach and blush roses from Gran's rose-bush outside and sit them in an empty cream bottle in the middle of the table. It looks nice, like a restaurant.

I keep my eyes away from Gran and what she's pushing around with her spatula in that pan.

"Okay," she says, handing me the bowl of rice and a bucket of margarine. "Put these on the table and call the family." She turns back to the cupboard and gets out her fancy company platter, the one she uses for the church ladies when they come to dinner. She slides my rattlesnake out of the pan and onto the platter. Then she shuffles over to the fridge, takes out a couple of leaves of lettuce, and uses them to decorate the sides of the plate. Which might not be strange for regular families, but let me tell you, Gran is not one for garnish.

"Go on, call them," Gran says, plopping the decorated platter of snake on the table. "And close your mouth, girl, you're catching flies." Then she winks at me. Gran *winks* at me! She's never done that before. Ever. I almost think I didn't see it, and maybe I didn't, because she's already turned back to the stove and is pouring the steaming-hot canned peas out of their pot and into a bowl.

I go into the living room where Mom is sitting between Tessa and Simon reading *The King's Stilts*. That book is way too young for Tessa, but she's pretending to be enraptured. I notice she has fallen back to using a cute little babyish voice, higher pitched than normal, which is really pathetic.

"Dinner's served," I say. Because what else can I do? I'm not going to tell them what dinner is. I'll leave that honor to Gran.

"Okay," Mom says, looking up and smiling, as if she didn't just yell at me half an hour ago. "Let's go, kids. I'll finish the book after dinner." She places the book face down on the coffee table, and I want to say, That's not good for the spine of the book. But I don't. I just turn and walk back down the hall and into the kitchen, where Gran, her apron hooked on the back of her chair, is already at the table. I sit. The rest of them come in like a party. Chattering, laughing. Gran perched at the head of the table like a spider in wait.

"Oh . . . smells good," Mom says in her company voice. "What's for dinner?"

"Snake," Gran says. She grabs my hand in her old gnarled one, Mom's hand in her other, and bows her head. Gran starts saying grace in her scratchy, worn voice before Mom can say tickityboo.

"Thank you, Lord, for all the blessings we enjoy. Our health, our eyesight, these children, and ah . . . eh" – a cough-snort that sounds seriously like a disguised laugh gets smothered in Gran's nose. I sneak my eyes open, glance sideways to see if it was, because Gran doesn't laugh much, and certainly not during grace. But I must have imagined it, because Gran's face seems dead serious, straight as a board – ". . . for the gift of this bountiful food. Amen."

"Amen," we say.

"Snake?" says Mom. "You're *kidding* me, right?"

"Nope," says Gran cheerfully, serving herself up a nice hot portion. "Jack?" She hands the platter of cooked rattle-snake to me, and I'm about to pass, but that's when Mom starts screaming.

"There is no way, you crazy old lady," Mom yells, her body jerking away from the table like that plate of snake is still alive, knocking over her chair, its wooden frame clattering noisily on the floor, "that I'm going to let you feed that to my children."

But Gran doesn't back down. She just sticks her chin out, in that stubborn way she has. "You walked away from your rights four and a half months ago, Fran. I'm taking care of these children the best I know how. Feeding them, clothing them, with limited resources. Rattlesnake's a good meal, healthy, nutri-tious, and, in some cultures, considered a delicacy. People pay big bucks to eat fresh rattlesnake, and thanks to Jack's largesse we got it for free."

"Jacqueline! Her name is *Jacqueline*. And no! We are not going to have that," Mom says, pointing at the snake. Her face red, chest puffed, arm stretched out, ending with her finger thrust forward like one of those fancy skinny dueling swords people fought with in the old days. "For . . . for dinner!" she sputters.

"Believe you me, Fran," Gran says calmly, "we're eating it."

I look at Mom, who left us here to rot. I look at Gran, who didn't want or expect us but picked up the pieces the best she could. I look down at that dressed-up platter of rattlesnake in my hand and, I swear, I wasn't planning on it, but I find myself scooping up a serving and putting it on my plate. I hand the platter to Tessa, who is sitting petrified in her chair. She squeaks and quickly passes the platter on to Simon, who looks down at it, scared. Then he looks up at me.

I smile at him, trying to let him know that he doesn't have to. I don't mind if he doesn't eat snake.

"Don't!" My mom says, her voice sharp. But Simon does. The brave little guy. He picks out a small piece of rattlesnake and drops it like a marble on his plate.

And we eat that snake. Me, Simon, and Gran. I could eat anything, even cow patties, if I had to. I could eat the moon. So proud of Simon, standing up to Mom like that, because you know what? She's never taking us back home with her. If she was going to, she would have already.

Dinner's good. Gran shows us how you've got to hold the snake in between your two hands. "Fingerfood," she calls it. "You eat it like a short cob of corn." And that's what we do. We bite our teeth in, right up against the backbone, because the snake is the meatiest there, and then once our teeth are set, we drag them down, toward the end of the skinny little rib bones, sucking the meat off as we go.

It tastes good, way better than I expected. And I don't know if it is so delicious because rattlesnake *is* delicious and it's my new favorite meal, or if it's because Gran, Simon, and me are eating it together. The three of us, united. Mom and Tessa watching, poking at their rice and canned peas, noses in the air.

● ● ● ●

Mom got in her dark-navy Jetta with its stereo, air conditioning, and all the bells and whistles, and drove away. Mom's car is clean and shiny. So different from Gran's rusted-out heap of junk held together with spit and a prayer. Gran's rattletrap is so rickety that we can see the ground whizzing by through the holes in the floorboard.

"Where'd you get this car?" I'd asked Mom as she was getting ready to leave.

"Oh," Mom said, waving a hand breezily in the air. "I borrowed it from a *friend*." And the way she said a *friend*, leaning on it slightly, a little smile on her lips, I knew the *friend* was a man. I don't know how Simon and Tessa feel about that, if they figured out what's going down, but I don't like it. Mom having a *friend*. A close-enough friend to lend her his very expensive recent-model car? What kind of bull is that?

"Do you think Dad is in heaven?" I said. To remind her that her husband died for our country. That it was not even a year ago that he was shot dead! I wanted her to remember that, before she went flouncing around with her new friend. "Do you think he watches over us?" I asked, smiling innocently. "That he can see everything we're thinking and doing?"

"You're hanging out with Gran too much," Mom said. "When you're dead, you're gone. Compost for the trees." That's what she said, but her voice, the expression on her face? It told a whole different story. So maybe she'll think twice before she goes flying about town with her boyfriends.

Anyway, she's gone now, and I hope what I said to her about Dad sticks.

"Bye," Mom had said, standing on the porch, her overnight bag in her hand, giving each of us a quick kiss and hug. She still smelled the same. Different, but the same. A quick hug and then it was over.

Us kids stood on the porch with our happy faces on, smiling and waving, slapping at mosquitoes that always seem to be more prevalent at that time of night. It's dusk and there we were, wearing our good clothes, hollering, "Good-bye," "I love you," hokey things like that, until Mom's car disappeared up and over the bend, in a cloud of dust, her arm sticking out of the window waving back and forth like a windup doll, until she was gone from sight.

And now here I am, lying in bed, stiff-bodied with rage, because Tessa is crying again. She's been going at it for more than an hour. I mean, come on! We're all sad, okay? It doesn't help for her to be blubbering up a storm. How's that making Simon feel? Or me, for that matter? Not too great. Selfish, is what it is. A few tears, okay, I understand, but these out-of-control hysterics are ridiculous!

And you know why she's crying? She's crying because Mom didn't take her home with her! "Why . . . didn't . . . Mom . . . take . . . m . . . me?" That's what she's crying! Not *Why didn't Mom take us?* No! It's *Why didn't Mom take me?*

I don't know why I didn't see it. Tessa was probably *happy* that Simon and I looked so bad! Less competition! That's why she was acting so sickly sweet the whole time Mom was here, following her everywhere, giggling at all her jokes with a laugh that any half-wit could tell was fake, playing with Mom's hair. Telling Mom, "You're soooo pretty!" "I love your dress!" "Where'd you get those shoes? They're divine!" *Divine!* Tessa probably doesn't even know what *divine* means.

I mean, what's she think? That Mom's going to take her off to live in the big city and leave me and Simon behind. I don't *think* so! Mom doesn't want Tessa any more than she wants the rest of us, and that's a fact. We would probably just cramp her wonderful single lifestyle.

Finally, I can't take these histrionics anymore.

I stomp over to Tessa's bed, yank the covers off her head. "Why are you crying?" I say in a cold voice.

"I . . . I . . . miss . . . my . . . ma . . . maaah!" Tessa's face all beet red and swollen with tears.

And I don't know what she is expecting. Sympathy? "*Shut* up! Just *shut* your stupid bawling face! We're *sick* and tired of hearing you cry! Right, Simon?" Simon doesn't say anything, but I didn't expect him to.

I glare at Tessa. "You aren't the *only* one, you know." My face is twisted up, sarcastic and mean. "You aren't the only child she's left! I hate to be the one to break the terrible news to you, but there are two more of us in the room. All of us have a dad who's dead and a mom who doesn't want us! Big deal! Do you see us bawling our heads off? *No!* You don't! So just *shut* up. *Shut* your big fat mouth or *I'll* shut it for you!" Then I throw the covers back over her stupid-looking head, with its fake, tired-out curls that look more stringy than luscious, and stomp back to my bed.

I lie in bed, angry. Tessa's trying to be quieter. Soft, stifled, hiccuping sobs, her face jammed into her pillow. But now

Simon is crying too. He probably thinks I'm mean. And I am. I don't care. So what. I'm a mean, cold bitch, and there's nothing anyone can do about it.

But I have to say, even though it felt good to be so mean to Tessa, it wasn't smart because now I've got weeping in symphony, dual-sound stereo. I lie there and listen to my brother and sister cry, my own eyes hot and bitter, fists clenched, hating my mom. Next time she comes, I'm not going to take a bath or brush my hair or anything. I'm not going to run out to the porch and say hello. Maybe I won't even bother to come down for an hour or two. I'll just stay upstairs in our bedroom, reading a book. "I don't care whether you're here or not. Actually, I'd prefer it if you don't come." That's what I'll say to her. "Messing up our lives. Just listen to them, Mom. Simon and Tessa are crying their eyes out, and all because you just can't be bothered!"

Mom thinks she's so great, but she's just stupid. Wafting in here with her beauty-parlor hair and her fancy French mani-cure. Only staying for an afternoon, like that's all the time she can spare. Criticizing Gran all the time, making her feel bad, when Gran's taking care of us the best that she can. I hate my mom. I really do.

● ● ● ●

My heart shakes me awake. It's pounding like a trapped bird in a cage. Something's wrong.

The room's dark. Not even a moon tonight. What's wrong? I ask myself. What's wrong? And then the answer drops into my head and down to my belly.

Tessa's gone.

I scramble out of my bed and run over to hers, stubbing my toe on something hard. I can't make out what. It's too dark. I hope I'm wrong, but my belly knows I'm not.

I get to her bed. It's empty.

"Tessa?" I whisper, rummaging through her bedclothes like somehow that will make her reappear. I want to yell her name loud, but I don't want to wake Simon and Gran.

"Tessa?" I check the bathroom, even though I know she's not there. I check the downstairs fast, just in case. But she's gone. I don't even bother with the henhouse and the barn. I know where she's heading. She's going to try to find Mom.

I shove my feet in my running shoes, grab a flashlight, and slip out the kitchen door. I make sure not to let the screen door slam behind me. Going out the front door would have been more efficient, but Gran's bedroom is right off the hall and I don't want to wake her up. Tessa running away is the last thing in the world I want Gran to know. She might have a heart attack, and then where would we be?

Once outside, I start running. I round the side of the house, my mind spinning. How long ago did she leave? Is it my fault? Of course it is, stupid! There was no reason to be so mean. I'm glad it's dark because I can feel the knowledge of this staining my face red.

Out on the driveway, I'm light-footed, running quiet until I get away from the house. Then I break into a dead run. The sound of my feet, the thumping of my heart, loud in my ears. The night seems so silent, like I'm the only living creature awake in the world.

I hear a rustling sound in the bushes.

"Tessa?" I say, swinging my flashlight in the direction of the noise. I catch glowing eyes in the beam of my light, but they're too low down and close together to be Tessa's. Besides, human eyes don't glow in the dark. Only animal's eyes do. They turn and disappear in the undergrowth, and the movement unfreezes me. I continue running.

"Tessa. . . ." I call softly. "Tessa?"

When I get to the end of the driveway, it's a no-brainer which way to go. I can still see Mom's car in my head, turning right, her matchstick arm waving out of the window.

I can yell loud now. I'm far enough away from the house for Gran not to hear.

"Tessa! *Tessa!*" I'm running fast and hard, but then my foot twists in a pothole that my flashlight didn't catch. It's not bad but it's enough to stop me in my tracks for a heartbeat or two.

"Tessa!" I yell. "*Tessa! Goddammit*, Tessa! Where *are* you?"

And that's when I hear it. The sound of running footsteps up ahead. While I'm standing in the middle of the road rotating my ankle, trying to get it in moving shape again. I get a real crazy idea, but I do it anyway because what do I have to lose? Tessa's a pretty good runner, and with my ankle a little funky . . .

"Ahh!" I scream at the top of my lungs. "Ow! Oh my God! Help!" I fall on the road clutching my ankle, rolling in the dirt. "Dammit! My ankle! I'm hurt!" I hope a car doesn't come and squash me flat like a bug. "Help me, Tessa! Pullease!" I wait and listen. I hear her footsteps falter, then stop. "Help! My foot! It hurts! It hurts!"

And that's all it takes. A few more groans and bellows and there she is helping me to get up off the ground. "Oh my God, thank you, Tessa! Thank you so much," I say, playing the wounded soldier very well.

"Here," she says, taking her backpack off and slinging it over her left shoulder so my arm can fit comfortably around her shoulders for support. "Is that okay? Can you walk on it?"

Now, to be honest, my ankle's a little sore, but I could most definitely walk it off and get back home.

"Ow! No," I say. "I can't seem to put my weight on it. I'm afraid I'm going to have to hop."

I hop for quite some time.

"Tessa, wait," I finally say, because this hopping is just ridiculous. My whole hopping leg is on fire. It's seizing up in cramps. And we're still not even one-third of the way up Gran's driveway. "I have to stop."

"Are you okay?" she says, her voice coming in puffs. She's sweating and breathing hard too because as I got more tired, I had to lean on her harder.

"Yeah. Let's sit for a minute." She helps me down.

"Here, Jack," she says. "You sit on my backpack. It will be more soft."

"Thanks," I say and sit down because if I'm sitting on her backpack full of things, she'll be less likely to run.

I have to admit, though, Tessa being so thoughtful doesn't help my guilt quotient any.

"Okay, Tessa, look," I say. "I'm going to be up front with you. My ankle's not hurt."

"What?" She looks confused.

"I mean, my ankle's hurt, but it's not hurt that bad."

"Wha . . . ?" She's being so dense.

"I can walk, Tessa. Okay? I twisted it but not that bad. Not fall-on-the-ground bad."

"But you did fall on the ground?"

"Yes, Tessa, I fell on the ground, but that was to get you to come back. I'm sorry. I couldn't think of anything else to do."

"You . . . you wanted me back?"

"Of course, Tessa. Of course I wanted you back! I was so scared when I woke up and you were gone."

"You were?"

"Yes, Tessa. Jeez. I was scared outta my friggin' skull!"

"You were?"

"Yes!" My voice is really loud now, almost yelling. But it's like I'm talking to a zombie. It's like she's just not getting what I'm saying, she's in a fog.

"But I thought you hated me. I thought you wanted me gone. I thought everybody would be better off without me. Gran doesn't like me."

"Yes, she does —"

Tessa cuts me off. "No, she doesn't. Don't lie. And you've always been Simon's favorite. Dad's too. Mom's the only one that liked me even a little, and now . . ." Tessa starts crying. "Now, even Mom's gone."

I had no idea she saw me as the golden child when I always thought she was. "Oh, Tessa," I say. I hold her in my arms and rub her back. "It's okay. Everything's going to be okay. I love you, Tessa. Honest, I do."

And when she finishes crying, we get up and walk on home.

● ● ● ●

"All right," Gran says at breakfast, rapping the table with her lumpy knuckles. "After the morning chores are done, we're going into town. You kids need your school supplies. Maybe not all of them, but we're going to get what we can manage. So clean up, wash up. Simon, have you fed the dog?"

"Yes, ma'am," Simon says, smiling proudly. "I already fed him, ma'am." His legs swinging.

"Good. Then you can help Jack with the dishes. Tessa, you get upstairs and make the beds." Tessa pulls a face at this one, but she slides off her chair and goes. I let Simon start clearing the table while I get a potholder and take the frying pan off the stove. Normally, I'd just wash the pan last, so it won't get the dishwater all disgusting until the end, but Simon's helping, and sometimes he forgets to grab things with potholders. He thinks because the stove's turned off that the pots and pans magically lose their heat. I can't tell you how many times he's burned his fingers, grabbing something off the stove. I scrape the dried-out egg scum off the sides into Tom's bowl. Yes, we had eggs again. We eat a lot of eggs. Scrambled eggs, boiled eggs, fried eggs. Which is why Tessa didn't argue about getting stuck on bed-making duty, because I could tell her mouth was full of soggy, wet eggs, all squidgy and warm. Gran does not tolerate wasting food.

Now before the other night and our conversation on the road, I might have said, Hey, Tessa, what's that you got in your mouth? Gran would have made her open it, and Tessa would have had to swallow those babies down and I would have laughed my guts out, but I don't do that anymore. I'm trying to be nicer.

It's kind of cozy this morning, doing cleanup with Simon, his little body perched companionably beside me on a kitchen chair. The two of us side by side, our hands slopping in warm dishwater. I've got him rinsing the dishes. Which is basically just a dip and plop. That's all he's got to do. But he takes it so seriously, wants to make sure he does it right. The pink tip of his tongue, caught between his teeth and sticking out of the corner of his mouth. You'd think he was doing rocket science, that's how focused he is.

When the cleanup is done, we go upstairs and change out of our home clothes. We wash our faces and I let Tessa braid my hair. And even though braids are not my thing and she's done them a little off kilter, I leave them in and tell Tessa they look pretty.

When we're all ready, we go outside and pile into Gran's car.

I laid a sheet of plywood along the car floor in the back a couple of days ago. I struggled with this decision because it's kind of fun when you're sitting in the backseat watching the ground whiz by. It's sort of like your own private TV show. But lately, I've started getting worried that one of those holes was going to open up wider and Tessa and Simon's feet would go crashing through. The image of that kept bonking me on the head until finally I went to Gran, we talked it over, I showed her the floor in the back. She was really surprised. I guess she'd never noticed before. She got me some plywood that was leaning up against the backside of the henhouse. I cut it and laid it down on the back floor of Gran's old rattletrap car.

"Hey!" Simon says when we get into the car. "What's this?"

"It's a board," I say.

"Well, take it away," he says, kicking at it. "It'll block our view."

"Yeah," says Tessa, like it was a dumb thing to do.

"It's staying," I say. "It's safer that way." They look like they want to argue, but I shut my face, so they know there's no point. And there's nothing they can do about it. I'm bigger than them, and Gran and I are in charge.

First stop, Pharmasave.

The school supplies list calls for specific things, like HB pencils #2 or four white erasers, fancy stuff like that. But Gran doesn't pay attention to the list.

"It's just a reference, a guideline, not the Bible," she says, tossing the bargain-brand equivalents into our shopping cart. She's trying to keep track of things, adding up the prices as she goes along, but she keeps losing her place and has to start adding the total up all over again.

She gets that way sometimes. She'll be doing something

and then she'll walk off and forget that she was doing it. Yesterday, I came downstairs and the stove burner was on. It must have been on all night because all around the stove it was hot like a furnace.

And now here we are in Pharmasave and the numbers and totals of things are slipping out of Gran's head and she's getting all grouchy and flustered, her face growing redder and redder by the minute. I want to offer to help, but I don't want Gran to know that I notice, because Gran's a really proud woman and it might make her embarrassed.

"Gran?" Tessa says. "Can I have one of these?"

I look over. Tessa's holding up one of those glittery girly-girl pens in pink. I'm just stunned. What is Tessa thinking, that we're made of money? She was there in that church along with the rest of us, watching that stupid collection plate go round. People gave up their hard-earned money so that we could buy the bare essentials. That's it. Not for frivolous roller pens!

"Come on, Gran. Please? I really, really love it. Ow! What'd you do that for?" The last bit is directed at me, because I'd just given her a sharp boot in the leg when Gran had turned her head. I'm trying to be nicer, but please. Enough is enough.

"Why'd you kick me?" Tessa says indignantly.

I'd tell her why, I'd give her an earful, no problem, but I don't want to shame Gran any more than we have to. So I just say, in a meaningful way, "*You know.*"

"No, I don't," Tessa says irritably, rubbing her shin like I kicked her oh-so-hard. But she puts the fancy pen back, so that's a small victory.

At the cashier, Gran pulls the brown paper bag with all the collection-plate money in it out of her purse and dumps the contents right there on the counter. None too quietly, I might add. It sounds like the whole store is coming down. She pushes her hair back out of her face, perches her bifocals on the end of her nose, and starts counting out the loonies, toonies, quarters, nickels, and dimes. Out loud! Carefully smoothing and laying the crinkled five-dollar bills out in a stack to the side.

There is a line forming behind us as Gran and the pimply faced cashier count out the mounds of change. It's taking forever! And it's too much for me to deal with. Someone we know might come in. I know it's weak, I know it's chicken, I know I should stand by Gran, proud and tall, but I don't. I grab Simon's hand, Tessa's too, say, "We'll meet you outside, Gran," and we abandon her in there, counting out the charity change.

We stand outside, two storefronts down, so no one can put two and two together. Nobody talking, too embarrassed and ashamed. Hot midday sun beating down on our heads.

• • • •

Serenity Valley has upped the campaign. There are glossy foldout flyers in the mailbox practically every week for me to bury deep in the garbage. It might seem wrong to be doing this, but Gran did tell them she wasn't interested. So, actually, I'm just saving her from getting irritated by too much junk mail. Besides, those flyers look pretty good, and I don't want Gran to be tempted.

And then there's stinky, old, monkey-faced Mr. Buchanan striding around the place, with his gray-suited crony taking notes. Walking around the property like he already owns it. Making his big development plans, when Gran hasn't even said yes!

When Gran's here, she runs them off the property. "Stop salivating. I'm not dead yet, Teddy!" she'll say, shooing her hands at him like he's a pesky mosquito. And when she's otherwise occupied, I send Tom out to pee on the wheels of their fancy Mercedes SUV.

● ● ● ●

"Simon." I'm trying to keep my voice calm, but it's getting frustrating. He's just not trying hard enough. "Simon?"

"Huh?" he says.

"Simon, I need you to focus!" I tap my finger on the book, right under the words he's supposed to be reading. "What's this say?"

"I don't know," he says. He's got that sullen look on his face. He's not even looking at the page. He's rumpling and unrumpling the blanket on his bed.

"Sound it out. I . . . would . . . not . . . could . . . not . . . Simon!"

"What?"

"Sound it out with me!" I could strangle him. Here we are with school starting tomorrow and he's not reading one smidgen better! A whole summer spent trying to teach him to read and it's just not working. "They're going to fail you, Simon, if you don't start trying! I swear to God. You have to focus. Okay?"

"Okay. . . ." he sighs heavily.

"Okay." I take a deep breath to calm myself. Me yelling at him doesn't help. It makes him shut down even further.

"Why don't you just leave him alone?" Tessa says. "Who cares if he can read?"

"You stay out of this!" It's easy for Tessa to say, sitting cross-legged on her bed, flying through *Emily of New Moon*. You would think, with her being such a good reader, that she'd realize how important it is for Simon to be able to read.

I turn back to him. "Okay, Simon, let's try it again. We'll start right here. See where my finger is? As I move my finger, we'll read the words, okay? Let's go."

"I . . . could . . . not . . . would . . . not . . . in . . . a . . . box," both of us reading. "I . . . could . . . not . . . would . . . not . . . with . . . a . . . fox."

"Good, Simon! Okay, now you try reading that again by yourself."

"What?"

"You try it by yourself." He looks hesitant. "Go on, you can do it." He scrubs at his eyes with his bunched-up fists.

"I'm tired," he says. "Can we stop now?"

"No, Simon, you have to read it by yourself. You want to be in third grade, don't you?" He nods. "Well, third-graders have to be able to read by themselves."

"But I'm tired," he says. "I'm tired . . . I'm tired!" I want to insist, but he does look tired. He has shadows under his eyes. He's probably just as nervous about going back to school as I am for him.

"You sure you don't want to try by yourself?" I'd really like him to try, but I don't want to push him and ruin his confidence before his first day of school.

"Yeah, I'm sure. I'm really, really sleepy. I want to go to bed."

"It's kind of early for bed."

"I don't care. I'm really tired."

"Okay," I say. "You can go to bed after we practice a little self-defense."

There's no problem with that. We go downstairs. Gran doesn't mind that we use the sofa cushion. Simon gets out of the headlock in two seconds flat and blocks my punches. Throws a few hard punches into the sofa cushion that I'm holding up at chest level, his face determined and rosy-cheeked, and Gran, sitting in her rocking chair, claps and cheers him on.

I think she's figured out why I punched that kid in the nose, and I can tell she approves of what I'm teaching Simon.

Tucking Simon into bed, I show him the inside of his running shoe for the umpteenth time. I've written Gran's phone number on the inside with a black permanent marker. Nice and thick so it won't wear out. I do this because along with the reading difficulties, Simon has trouble remembering numbers. He still doesn't know our address or telephone number. And with me being at a different school, who's to say he's not going to get on the wrong bus accidentally, because he reverses numbers all the time. He could read the number six bus and think it's the number nine and end up who knows where. I've asked Tessa to make sure he gets on the right one, but she's unreliable. Sort of like Mom.

"Okay, Simon, what's this?"

"Um . . . my shoe?" he says, eyes twinkling. He's happy now that the schoolwork is done.

"No, Simon!" I say sternly, because this is no joking matter.

"It's *not* my shoe?" Simon says, glancing around at an imaginary audience. "Hmm . . . how strange?"

"Simon, you *know* what I mean." I'm trying not to laugh because he is really quite funny.

"It looks like my shoe." He takes it from me and sticks his nose inside it, takes a good long whiff. "Phuffee! It *smells* like my shoe." Tessa's giggling. He's about to lick it, but I take it away. The things that kid will do for a laugh.

"I've written our phone number," I say, "on the –"

"I know, Jack. *Jeez!*" he says, suddenly irritable. "You've told me once if you've told me a million times! It's our phone number. You've written it on the inside of my shoe, so if I have an emergency or get lost, or take the wrong bus home, I can take my shoe off and show it to someone so that they can call home. I'm sure they will enjoy participating in that." Tessa's giggling again. Egging him on. "Especially rummaging around the inside of my smelly shoe for our phone number."

"Fine," I say. He gets in bed, and I go downstairs to scrub out the lasagna pan I left soaking.

As I'm cleaning the pan, I'm worrying about Simon, but I'm worrying about me too. Hoping that the cute top I got at the Sally Ann with Gran, the one with the flowing sleeves, didn't belong to Miss Popular last year. And if it did, I hope she doesn't recognize it and squeal, "Oh look, everybody! That girl is wearing my old top from last year! Oh my! She must have bought it from the Salvation Army, where I donated it last spring." It might seem like an insignificant thing to worry about, given all the other troubles we've got. But I do. Leave it to me and I'll worry about anything. I'm an expert worrier.

But Simon's my biggest worry by far. And I pray, I pray hard, not just on Sunday. I pray every night now, after the others are asleep. I get out of bed, kneel down on the floor, and put my hands in praying position, because I figure, if I'm going to pray, if it has to be heartfelt, I might as well do it right. Just in case God decides, for once, to take a coffee break from the real problems of the world and is sitting back eating a donut and he happens to hear my prayer.

I know the chances of that occurring are about one in a billion, but just in case, I do the whole drill, on my knees, my head bowed, my hands together and making a steeple. I send up prayers for my brother, Simon. That God keeps him safe and gets him on the right bus. I pray for him to turn the switch in Simon's brain so he can learn like other kids do. I always add a prayer for Gran, to keep her health and not to sell the farm. And ever since Tessa ran away, I've started adding her in my prayers too. I never did before, because I didn't know she needed it, but I do now, and I think it helps.

I pray long and hard tonight. Longer than usual. Then I crawl back into my bed and fall asleep.

● ● ● ●

AUTUMN

First day of school and I'm finding it hard to concentrate because I'm worrying about Simon so much. Which is not good. This school is enormous and I keep getting lost. It's ten times bigger than the elementary school. And you have to change classes every single period, and there's this big noisy buzzer that blasts at the beginning of one class and the end of the other, and every time it goes off, it startles me. I suppose it's because I'm not expecting it. I'm trying hard not to jump, because when I do, people laugh. But it's difficult to know exactly when the buzzer's going to go. It's like somebody popping out of a closet in the dark. It's impossible not to yelp.

Then, once the buzzer goes, it's like a mad dash, because I've only got a couple of minutes to find my way to my next classroom, which always seems to be in the opposite section of the school. And the map they gave me doesn't make sense. I don't think there is any way I'm ever going to figure it out. I'm not a stupid person, but the layout of this school is impossible.

So here I am, staggering into class, with my growing stack of books. Late. Luckily, I'm not the only one. Other kids seem to be confused, arriving even later than me, looking embarrassed, cheeks red, head tucked. The teachers pass out more and more textbooks. You're supposed to put them in your locker, but I don't have a combination lock. The homeroom teacher said that if you don't have a lock you should buy one at the office, but I didn't have the money, so I have to carry my books everywhere because the teacher said if we lose any of our textbooks we're going to have to pay for them and I'm sure, with these books being so thick, that replacing them wouldn't be cheap so that's another necessity I'm going to have to hit Gran up for. A combination lock. I hate asking Gran for money.

At lunchtime, I follow the crowd and end up in the cafeteria. It smells so good. They're serving pizza. I haven't had pizza since Dad died. They've got a snack bar where they're selling ice cream and soda and potato chips, food I used to take for granted in my old life. My mouth is watering. It's hard to concentrate with everyone chowing down on all that tasty food. Hard to chew and swallow my peanut-butter sandwich. Hard to pretend I like it. And all around me people are throwing food away too. Whole trays of food, most of it untouched. Food that I would leap at now, if I had the chance.

Not that I would, of course. I have food. Perfectly good

food. And when I finish this peanut-butter sandwich, if I'm still hungry, no problem, I have another one in my lunch sack, and an apple from our tree. It's small, and doesn't look perfect and shiny like the store-bought ones, but it has good flavor. It's apple season now, so the apples are really good, have a nice crisp texture, and are full of sweet autumn-time taste.

I'm lucky. No feeling sorry for myself, sitting here alone at the end of a rectangular bench, eating my lunch. I see a couple of people from last year's class passing in the halls every now and then. I'm sure they're somewhere in this lunchroom, but I'm not about to look. I don't want to seem eager. Besides, even if I did see someone who was in the other school, why would they want to eat lunch with me? I never ate lunch with any of them before. I honestly didn't think we were going to be staying here. Saw no point in trying to make friends.

All of a sudden I get a flash of my old friends, the ones I had back in St. John's, when I had a normal life, complete with regular store-bought clothes, a mom and a dad, and an allowance.

Emily, Morgan, and Liz. I wonder what they're doing. If they're all still best friends. If they miss me. I wonder if they still have sleepovers with popcorn and rented videos. And it's like I'm a movie camera for a moment. I can see their wide-open faces, crowding in toward the lens. It's like they're right there, on the other side of a mirror from me, and they're laughing and laughing and having such a good time. Arms around one another's shoulders, pulled together close, telling secrets, sharing lives and stories. And I get a lump in my throat, missing that old life. I can't swallow my sandwich past the longing. So I stand up, pick up my gargantuan stack of textbooks and school supplies, toss the rest of my sandwich into the gray garbage bin. I toss away good food like the rest of the kids and go out into the glossy-floored high-school hall.

● ● ● ●

When the bus drops me off, I walk fast. I try not to run. Hoping Simon did okay and got home safely, I go up the back steps, kick off my shoes, shove them into the box, go into the kitchen, and thank God! There's Simon. He's sitting at the kitchen table with Tessa. He's got his workbook open. His pencil is gripped in his hand in the funny way he has, halfway between proper pencil-holding and a fist. He made it home! I'm so relieved to see him. My eyes travel over him, looking for scrapes or new blossoming bruises, but there don't seem to be any. And for the first time today, I find myself letting out that breath I was holding.

"Hey, little dude," I say. "How was school?"

"Fine," he says.

"How was your teacher?"

"Okay."

"Who'd you get?"

"Jack! I'm trying to do my homework here!" he says, looking up at me with a scowl.

"Right you are," I say. "I better get started myself." I unload my books on the kitchen table and shake out my arms because they're tired and sore from lugging my stuff around all day. Gran's at the stove cooking dinner, and from the smell of it, I think she's making her world-famous oven-fried chicken. Gran makes the best oven-fried chicken in the world. Hands down. "Smells fantastic, Gran," I say.

Simon's okay. He has survived his first day of school. He caught the bus home with Tessa, no problem. They are here safe and sound. And suddenly, I feel like the world is spinning properly again. It's back on its axis, momentarily perhaps, but it doesn't seem to be wobbling quite as precariously as it has for the last week or so. My appetite roars back into my belly with a vengeance, and I am ravenously hungry.

Gran doesn't say anything, just grunts and takes out her metal mixing bowl, setting it on the counter. I don't know what she's going to whip up in that, but it's bound to be delicious. "What are you making in that bowl, Gran?" I say. I like to know what we're having for dinner. Then I can daydream about it, get my belly and my mouth all ready for the taste.

"Buttermilk biscuits."

"Oh, Mama!" Gran's buttermilk biscuits are to die for. Add a little margarine and a bit of honey. Piping hot, there's nothing better in this world.

"Gran," I say, feeling magnanimous. "You're the best damned cook in the whole world!"

"Don't swear, child!"

"Sorry." And then I remember about the combination lock, that I need the money. I don't want to say it right now, even though it just popped into my head. I think, I'll wait until later, so Gran doesn't think I was praising her cooking to butter her up.

But then I realize that to wait might be a sneaky thing to do, manipulative and untruthful. Gran deserves better than that. I remembered, so I should say it, straight up.

"Gran," I say. "I need money to buy a combination lock."

She doesn't answer right away, just keeps cutting the shortening into the flour for the biscuits.

"I need it for my locker. Otherwise somebody might steal my textbooks and I'll have to pay for them and that will cost more." Gran still doesn't answer, "Did you hear me?" I say.

Gran stops working the pastry cutter. It bangs on the side of the bowl. Simon and Tessa look up.

"How much?" she says finally.

"Four ninety-five. Do you have it?"

Gran sighs, turns back to mixing, "I'll manage."

"I need some new gym shoes," Tessa pipes up. "Mine are getting too tight."

"You should have thought of that when we were at the Sally Ann," Gran says. "They'll have to wait until next time."

Tessa opens her mouth to argue, but I cut her off. I don't want her screwing up my combination lock money.

"Tessa," I say. "Gran doesn't have that kind of money to throw around. Why don't you ask Mom? She said she was going to come up for my birthday next week. You could ask her then. Maybe she'll even take you into town in that fancy car of hers to buy you some new ones." I can tell Tessa likes that idea, because she gets back to her homework with a little smile on her face.

Dinner's good. Sitting around the table, seeing the faces of my family. Gran, my brother, my sister, and me, all eating good food, Tessa chattering happily about her day, her friends, the new teacher who she loves.

After the dinner cleanup, I go outside. It's still light out, but the days are getting shorter. Not quite as light as it was last week, or the week before. A gradual dimming of the day that occurs earlier and earlier.

When I'm in the house with a full belly of food and all the dishes and homework are done, I don't want to have to go out and put the chickens away, pick up any late-laying eggs, or lock up the henhouse. I don't want to put Bess in her stall and slide the barn door shut. It seems like a big hassle. I'd rather sit myself down with my brother and sister to watch a little *Friends* or *The Simpsons*. Not that I love either show, but there's something relaxing about zoning out in front of the TV and not doing anything. Not having to think or talk or work. Just sit there and watch the tube and laugh occasionally.

But once I'm outside and away from the suction pull of the TV, I find I'm glad that I am. The earth smells different at dusk. Dusk and dawn. Everything is more fragrant then, more alive and tingly with possibilities and promise.

After I lock up the chickens and the cow, I decide to climb the hill out back because sometimes you can get a mingling of both the worlds. Not for long, just a half an hour or so, when you can sometimes see the sun going down and the moon rising all at the same time. Both of them hanging, hovering in the opposite ends of the sky at once.

It doesn't happen often, but it does tonight. The moon is full. A round, glowing, smiling sphere, it's just coming up over the horizon as I arrive at the top of the hill. I lie down on my back, the sweet smell of late-summer grass filling my heart, my arms and legs spread wide, like a human X-marks-the-spot. I don't know why I feel the need to lie like this. Maybe it's so I can catch more of the beauty.

The warmth of the day wears off, giving way to the chill of the night. I watch the moon peek her glorious face up over the tips of the trees and then get more brave, showing more of her splendor until, finally, her radiant glow reminds the sun that it's night, and the sun streaks the sky with her brilliant song, until, finally, she can put it off no longer and sinks, slowly, below the opposite horizon. The sun disappears to bring day to another part of the world as the moon rises higher and higher into the darkening sky, calling out the stars to join in her dance.

● ● ● ●

When the alarm clock jangles me awake, at first it just seems like another morning. I shake Simon and Tessa awake. They crawl out of bed sleepy-eyed into the bathroom to brush their teeth.

"Happy . . . birthday, Jack," Simon says, muffling a yawn.

"Yeah . . . happy birthday," says Tessa, rubbing her eyes, smiling at me. "And Mom comes today too. Two good things at once."

"Oh yeah! Mom comes today," Simon says with a foamy toothpaste grin. As I stand there stunned.

I can't believe I didn't remember it was my birthday this morning right off the bat. I mean, I've been looking forward to this birthday my whole life! I'm thirteen! A teenager. Not a "tweenie." A *real* genuine teenager. And all of a sudden, I feel different than I felt a couple of seconds ago. More grown-up. So I don't jump around, leap from bed to bed like they are trampolines, beating my chest like Tarzan and screaming,

"Yahooooeee!" I just smile at my little brother and sister in a mysterious, teenagerly sort of way. "Why, thank you," I say. "How kind."

When I get downstairs, Gran's already in the kitchen at the stove. "Happy birthday, Jack," she grunts as I pass through on my way to the back porch.

"Thank you," I reply, pulling on my rubber boots over my pajamas. I don't bother getting dressed until after the chores. This way, I don't risk getting my school clothes dirty.

It smells like Gran is making buttermilk pancakes for my birthday breakfast. I tromp out to the barn and get the open bag of chicken feed from the storage shed, then it's back outside to the henhouse. I unlatch the door and watch the chickens come tumbling out. Coconut Zigzag, her little fluffy chicks, and one large fuzzy duckling towering over the chicks, bringing up the rear. That's another thing I admire about Coconut Zigzag, she doesn't play favorites. She's nothing like the animals in that book *The Ugly Duckling*. Coconut loves that duckling just as much as her other chicks. Around a week and a half after those eggs hatched, she proved it. She proudly marched her babies down to the pond for a drink, the duckling drank at the water's edge, just like her other children, and then, plop, hopped into the pond and began paddling in, with a little "peep . . . peep . . . peep."

Well, Coconut Zigzag went crazy out of her head with

worry, running around the water's edge, calling frantically to her baby, clucking and squawking. All the other chickens came running to see what the commotion was about, as the little duckling paddled farther and farther out. Finally, as a last resort, Coconut jumped into the pond. I don't know how she managed to do this because, logistically, chickens aren't able to swim. They aren't built for it, but somehow Coconut Zigzag managed to get to the duckling, who was by then about one-third of the way to the pond's center. She turned that duckling around and got him back to shore. A super-heroic effort! Well, what did that little fluffball duckling do once Coconut got him safely to shore? Darned if he didn't hop back into the pond two seconds later and start paddling out to the center again. Coconut, tired as she was, got her waterlogged body back into the pond and corralled him out again, collapsing when she got to shore in an exhausted, sodden heap of wet feathers and bone. "Peep . . . peep . . . peep . . ." went the duckling baby and, zoop, back into the water. And poor Coconut was lying there, panting on the shore, half dead. She raised her weary head, gave one squawk, and dropped it down to the ground again, her other chicks cheep-cheeping around.

That's the kind of mother she is. A good one. Almost killed herself to save her child. Not even her natural-born child, an adopted one. She would have gone after him again and again, if it hadn't almost killed her. It was a good thing she was too worn out to go after him again, because she probably would have drowned and the duckling was happy. Coconut Zigzag, lying there on the shore with all her little chicks peeping and fussing and pecking around her, probably realized that not only did one of her chicks look different, but it also acted different, and it could swim. She accepted the difference. Every day now, when Coconut and her brood go down to the pond for water, the little duckling will hop in for a swim and she lets him, watching safely, with her other chicks, from the shore.

"It's my birthday," I tell Coconut Zigzag and her chicks as they come out the door. "And my mom's coming for my birthday party." The chicks are too little to understand, but Coconut tilts her head to the side and fixes her eye on me as if to say, "Well, I'll be. Happy birthday, Jack."

Because it's my birthday, I want everybody to be happy and have a celebration, so I fling out a few extra fistfuls of feed for the chickens. When I go in to milk Bess, I give her an extra scoop of grain in her trough and I don't hear any complaining. She just hustles her butt over there and starts munching it up before I change my mind. Her tail lazily flicking up to shoo an errant fly off her hind quarters.

I'm a much faster milker than I used to be. I get Bess milked and stripped in about half the time it used to take me. I'm a regular little milking fiend.

Back at the house, Tessa and Simon are already tucking in

to breakfast. It is pancakes, and as I'm pulling off my boots, Gran's flipping a big stack of them on a plate for me. I carry the bucket of warm, foamy milk over to the counter by the fridge. I eat the pancakes while Gran strains the milk. Then we'll let it sit for a while, so the heavy cream can rise and we'll skim some off, to use for other things. Not too much, though, because then the milk can get too watery. It gets bland and tasteless. We just skim enough and save it up for something special. A special treat, like maybe some homemade ice cream for my birthday.

After I eat, it's upstairs to get dressed. Simon and Tessa are already dressed. They're in the kitchen now, doing the breakfast cleanup before they catch their bus.

I dress carefully, put on my new-to-me pretty blue top with the flowy sleeves. I've worn it once before. A trial run, and nobody came up to me and claimed it as their old top, which was good. And the more I think about it, the dumber that worry is anyway, because if you look in any normal store, they don't just sell one of anything. They have many of each item lined up in a row. They might have ten of the same shirt, several in each size and color. So who's to say I hadn't bought one of those tops, whenever the store was selling them new. There is no way anyone could tell if I was wearing their old top unless it had a distinctive rip or stain on it. And really! I'm not about to spend Gran's hard-earned money on something that has either a rip or a stain. I check the clothes over carefully. I'm not a fool.

I brush my hair good and hard, put on clean jeans. I take a bit more care than I usually do. I figure it's time. I mean, I'll never get like Tessa or Mom, but a little extra attention wouldn't hurt. I am a teenager and pretty soon I'll be doing teenager things, like going to dances and on dates. Going to the movies with the gang. But first things first. Before I start planning what I'm going to do with the gang, I better be a little more realistic. I don't need a lot, one friend would do me. Like today, for instance. It would be nice to go to school and have somebody say, "Hey, Jack, happy birthday."

Actually, I'd settle for somebody saying, "Hey, Jack." Just to have somebody other than a teacher say my name in a friendly way would be enough. Sometimes I feel like a ghost in this big school. Like I'm insubstantial, like the mist, don't exist. Like I could live or die and nobody would know the difference. They wouldn't be sad, or happy. It would just be meaningless to them. They'd have no reference point. "Jack Cooper?" they'd say. "Who's that? A boy? A girl? Really? Hmm. No, I don't think I ever saw her."

Nothing much happens at school this morning. Just the regular old regular. Not a birthdaylike day at all, but that's okay. I keep thinking about my family and the party we're going to have when I get home. It's going to be great. I'm glad Mom's coming. The kids have been missing her something fierce.

On the bus ride home, this girl asks, "Is this seat taken?" I shake my head and scoot over.

She sits down. I don't talk to her, and she doesn't talk to me, but I also don't turn my back to her and glue my face to the window.

The bus is in its usual state of chaos. The bus driver has no control. Kids are throwing things, bum-rapping people off their seats. Guys are swatting the popular girls over the heads with their books. A few guys two seats down are doing the old turn-the-eyelids-inside-out-to-impress-the-girls.

"Look at that," the girl says, nudging me.

"I know," I make my voice sound slightly bored. "So *grade* school."

"Yeah," she says, and we smile at each other, feeling sorry for these boys.

"I'm Kate." She extends her hand. It's freckled too. I shake it like we're grown-ups meeting on a train.

"Jack," I say. "Short for Jacqueline, but you can call me Jack." I use the take-it-or-leave-it attitude, all casual, like I'm Jack Nicholson speaking my cool movie dialogue.

"Jack," she says, like she's tasting it on her tongue. She smiles at me. "I like it."

I smile back. We glance at the eyelid boys, who now have their left hands slid under their shirts and tucked into their right armpits. They are making farting noises by cranking their bent right arms vigorously up and down.

"Give me a break," I say, rolling my eyes, even though I was teaching Simon how to do that very trick this summer.

Not that I think making farting noises is so "cool." I don't. But it's all part of my help-make-Simon-more-normal campaign. Boys of Simon's age find farting armpits hilarious. You have to be able to do it.

"Boys," Kate says, tossing her curly fire-engine hair.

"Boys," I say, tossing mine. "Can't live with 'em. Can't live without 'em." I stand up, even though the bus is moving and we're supposed to stay seated, and squeeze the metal tabs on either side of the window to open it wide and let the air blast in.

"Ah, that's better," I say, the hot outside air rushing past my face. I've started up a miniature revolution, I think, because everyone else starts standing up and opening their windows too. And even though the bus driver is bellowing, "Sit down! Sit down in your seats!" everybody ignores him because they want fresh air. We're tired of the oxygen-depleted, stale-sandwich, body-odor, and old-runner smell of the bus. Once it starts, there's no stopping the tidal wave of students opening wide every last window on the bus.

And it feels good, just being me. Jack. Not anybody's big sister, trying to be a good example. In this moment, I'm just

Jack. An individual, not a person with all these appendages hanging on and depending on me to keep the family together. It's such a good feeling, makes me grin, the wind blasting my hair back behind me like streamers on a bike. I want to say with a big Jack-Nicholson-in-*The-Shining* grin, "I'm. . . . baaaaaack!"

I saw that movie at a sleepover at my old friend Emily's house back in St. John's. We weren't supposed to watch it. Her mom had rented *Beauty and the Beast*, but when Emily's parents had gone to bed, we watched *The Shining* instead. It scared the hell out of us. Everybody was hiding their eyes. But I didn't. I forced myself to watch the whole movie from start to finish. I was the only one who managed and it made me feel brave. Like I was a gunslinger out in the Wild West and had just accumulated another notch on my worn leather belt.

"This is my stop," Kate says as the bus grinds to a halt, dust billowing in through the open windows, because we're on the High Road now. No asphalt here, just dirt and gravel. She gets up and says, "See you tomorrow."

I say, "Sure," like it's no big deal. She gets off the bus with about five other kids. They scatter as the bus door groans shut, the air brakes release, and the bus pulls back out from the side of the road and starts rumbling along toward my home again. And I can't help it. I'm smiling big all the rest of the way.

• • • •

Tessa and Simon are waiting by the mailbox when my bus pulls up. They are dancing around, excited to see me, and it feels good. Simon grabs my backpack and insists on carrying it, even though it has to be at least as heavy as he is.

"No. It's your birthday!" he says. "I want to carry it for you." It seems important for him to do this for me, so I let him. Even though I'm a little worried that it's going to be too heavy for him to manage the whole way, he does it, his legs bowing slightly from the weight and his body bent over almost in two.

By the time we get inside to the kitchen, his face is beet red and sweating. He deposits my backpack with a thud to the table. "There," he gasps out, breathing hard. "I . . . did . . . it! I carried . . . your . . . backpack for you! Happy . . . birthday . . . Jack!"

"Thank you!" I say. "Wow!" I make a real big deal about what he's done. "You're strong! That backpack is even hard for *me* to manage! You're growing up to be quite a man, Simon. Dad would be so proud of you." His chest puffs up like a little rooster right before it crows.

"Ah," he says. "It was nothing. It wasn't even hard! I'll carry your backpack anytime, Jack."

I ruffle his hair. I don't think Mom's here yet. I didn't see her car in the driveway. Unless of course, she forgot something, birthday candles maybe, and had to drive into town to get them. A last-minute emergency.

Just in case Tessa and Simon have something special planned with Mom, I don't say, "Mom here?" or anything like that. I don't want to ruin the big reveal.

I just glance around casually, for clues. I'm good at clues.

I pick up on things other people might miss, like right now, the pantry door is ajar. Mom might be in there. She might have hidden the car out back behind the barn.

"Hmm," I say. "I think I'll have myself some peanut butter and crackers. I'm a little hungry." I amble over to the cracked-open pantry door, ready to jump in the air and look surprised and fooled. I can already see the expression on Simon's face when I pretend to be startled. I fling the pantry door open a little wider than I usually would, so there'll be a better show for the kids. But I guess I didn't need to, because there's nothing in the pantry but food. I don't really feel like peanut butter and crackers, that was just a ruse. I'm feeling kind of foolish now, talking in that stupid, hearty getting-ready-to-be-fooled voice.

I make myself a couple of crackers with peanut butter and eat them too, even though I should be saving myself for cake.

Gran holds off dinner as long as humanly possible, but finally she says, "I'm sorry, Jack, we can't wait any longer. These pork chops are going to be dry as dust." Pulling the dinner out of the oven, poking at the food with her spatula.

"Fine, Gran. No big deal," I say, smiling broadly at Simon and Tessa. "Mom probably got caught up in traffic is all."

"She is on her way, though, right, Gran?" Simon asks for the millionth time, his face all scrunched and worried.

"Of course she's coming," Tessa says. "She promised. She wouldn't break her promise. And besides, it's not like it's just Sunday dinner. It's Jack's birthday party. Mom wouldn't miss that, right, Gran?"

"I called her apartment," Gran says wearily. "She wasn't picking up the phone, so I figured she was on her way. But she should have been here by now, so I don't know. We'll just have to start dinner without her."

Gran serves up the birthday food. It's one of her specialties, pork chops baked with fresh apples from our tree, and a little brown sugar and bacon. She made up the recipe, and it's usually really delicious. But today . . . Well, it had been baking a good hour longer than it should have, so the flavor's still there, but the meat is very dry. Even with the apples and the sauce. It's like chewing on stale cardboard. Which is a shame, because we don't get fancy food like pork chops very often. So when we do get to eat them, it would be nice if they weren't ruined waiting for someone who can't be bothered to be on time.

The meal is pretty silent. All of our ears waiting for the

sound of Mom's car. We pretend every now and then to have a conversation, but it doesn't work.

Dinner is done. We save the cake. Simon and Tessa do the dinner cleanup on their own, because it's my birthday. Gran's gone into the hall to the phone, to give Mom another try. I sit at the table to do my homework. "So it will be out of the way for when Mom gets here," I say, trying to keep Tessa and Simon's hopes up.

"Yeah," Tessa says. "Good idea." But she's white-faced and worried. None of us are talking about what's really on our minds. All of us are imagining all kinds of things, automobile accidents, bridges collapsing, murderers leaping out from dark alleys with gleaming knives in their hands.

We listen to Gran fumble through her address book. We hear her pick up the phone and the rrrrrr . . . rrrrrrrr . . . rrr . . . noise the old black phone makes as Gran dials the number. Collectively we hold our breath, even the clatter of the dish-washing has stopped. All of us wanting Mom to be there because then that means she's safe. Not wanting Mom to pick up the phone, because then that means she's not going to be bursting in through the front door at any moment.

"Hello," says Gran. Then, "Dammit all to hell, Fran! Where are you?"

I feel Simon and Tessa's eyes on me, but I study my math-book hard, like I'm really interested in my homework. Like I can actually see what's written on the page instead of this flood of sadness and smallness and disappointment washing over me. My mom's not coming. She couldn't be bothered to come for my birthday.

I hear Gran yelling now. "That's a bunch of bull! It's your daughter's birthday! How dare you forget! You let these kids down! No! You tell me, Fran. What am I supposed to tell them?"

There is a pause in Gran's cursing. She's listening, I suppose, to Mom and her lukewarm excuses. Then Gran starts up again, softer this time, but fierce, and we can hear her, even though she's trying to keep it down. "No bloody way! I don't care what kind of day you had, you get into that car and you –"

Listening to Gran, suddenly I get mad. So angry I'm really scared I'm going to explode, like a stick of lit dynamite has been jammed down my throat and is going to blast me into a million pieces. "It's okay, Gran!" I yell. "Tell her not to bother! I don't care!" I slam the hall door shut, good and hard, so Mom can't help but hear it on the other end of the phone. Then I'm out on the back porch.

"Where . . . where are . . . you going, Jack?" Simon comes after me, pulling on my hand. I want to shove him off, but I don't. I just pull on my boots, keep my head tucked down, hair falling forward so he can't see my face. Don't want him to see me crying.

"I'm . . . going . . . to put the chickens away. I'll . . . I'll be back. Just have to put the chickens away . . . so the fox won't get them. We'll have my cake when I get back."

And I'm gone out the door, moving quick, so he can't get his boots and come with me. I really need to be on my own.

I don't go to the henhouse right away. I need to run farther, my boots slapping hard against my bare calves.

I run until my body won't run any farther and stumbles me face first into the ground. There's something about falling that makes me unable to fight it anymore. I can't help it. Everything's just too much. The whole last year comes roaring out of me like a tidal wave. I hate it that I'm crying like my stupid mom matters when she doesn't, and I slam my clenched-up fists into the ground over and over until they're too bruised and sore to punch anymore.

When I get back to the house, night's fallen. I can see through the porch door that my family is waiting for me around the kitchen table, Gran, Simon, and Tessa. Warm golden light streams out the window, sending patches of rectangular light across the backyard. I don't want to go in. I get closer, and I can see my birthday cake on the table in front of them with thirteen candles in it, waiting to be lit. Even though it's dark and the evening chill is in the air, I find my footsteps coming slower and slower. I want to stay outside all night. I want to make my bed in the woods, cover myself in a blanket of leaves, make my life go away. But I can't. They are waiting.

I make my way to the henhouse. The chickens are all in. One or two heads turn toward me as I reach the door, but mostly the chickens just fluff up their feathers, shift a little in their sleep. I shut the door and set the latch. Then I move on to the barn. Bess is already there. Her head swings toward me. I give her a pat, drape my body against her side. I breathe in her warm, comforting, animal-milk smell. I would stay in here longer with her, but my family is waiting for me, so I don't.

When I come up the back porch steps, I'm still in darkness, but their faces turn toward the sound of my feet. I put a smile on my face as I step out of the night and into the glare of the overhead light. "Hi," I say, kicking off my boots, squinting slightly as my swollen eyes adjust to the sudden illumination. "Oh great! Cake!" I say. "It's so pretty! What kind is it, Gran?"

She says, "Sponge."

"Yum . . . My favorite." I give her a hug. I keep my body busy, my voice bright. "Just have to wash my hands. Chickens and cows and who knows what else," I say. "Be back in a second."

I wash my face. My hands especially are filthy. I use lots of hot water and soap. There's nothing I can do about my red-rimmed eyes, but I brush my hair, change my top, and then go back downstairs.

Gran lights the birthday candles on the cake. I make a wish. It's a good one. I'm not telling what it is, because even though I don't really believe in wishes coming true, it's better to be on the safe side.

The cake is good, and Gran made wild-strawberry ice cream too.

Then it's time for my presents. Simon gives me an O'Henry bar, which is my favorite. And he gives me this card he made. It's so beautiful. He used red construction paper and three kinds of glitter and it's in the shape of a heart, and he's drawn stick figures of me and him holding hands with big smiles on our enormous heads and wrote I LUV MI SITR! on it. I tell him, "I'm going to pin it right over my bed so I'll see it every night before I go to sleep." I will too, because it's obvious a lot of work went into that card, especially given how hard it is for him to print, draw, or cut things. And he did all three, for me.

When I open Tessa's present I can't believe it. Lying there is the sparkly pen she wanted so much at Pharmasave! She bought it for me with some of her egg money she had saved in the bank. The pen she wanted! So that's really nice. "I'll let you borrow it, Tessa," I say. "One day a week," because it's a generous gift and I think she should be rewarded for putting someone other than herself first. She's really learning, Tessa.

Then Gran says, "Okay, Jack, here you go," and she pulls a package out from under her yarn in her knitting basket! I had no idea she had something hidden in there. I unwrap Gran's present, and Gran got me the shoes I've been daydreaming

193

about but never thought I'd be able to have. When I saw them in the store, I didn't even bother to try them on, or check the price. I had just touched them and held them up to feel the softness of the fake suede against my cheek. Gran was busy at the checkout counter, so I don't know how she knew about these shoes. I certainly wouldn't have admired them if I'd thought she was watching.

I dance around the room with my brand-new shoes on my hands like mittens! Real teenager shoes. They have a slight platform and everything. Beautiful shoes and they're mine. Can't help myself, I kiss them, even though I know it's a weird thing to do.

"Try them on," Gran says. Her wrinkly face is smiling big too. I put them on and they fit me perfect!

"How did you do it, Gran?" I say.

Tessa leaps off her chair, waving her arms like windmills. "I snuck your shoes out of our room when you were in the bath –"

"I kept watch!" Simon pipes up.

"And Gran wrote down the size and then the lady at the store upped it one because us kids are growing so fast." And, "Can I have them after you outgrow them, Jack? Can I?"

"Of course."

So, my birthday was pretty good, all things considered. I go to bed thinking about how lucky I am. I have a lot to be grateful for. I think about school today, and the bus ride home.

The red-haired girl, Kate. How she said, "See you tomorrow."

I listen to the snuffling sleep noises Simon makes, like a small animal nuzzling at its mother's side for milk. Tessa is snoring softly, even though she insists she doesn't. I think of Mom. My mind can't help but go to that, but when it does I steer it away, because Mom doesn't deserve my thoughts. I make my mind think of happier things, my brother and sister and Gran too. I have Tessa's pen in my hand, pulled in close to my chest, right next to Dad's watch hanging on its string. I've pinned Simon's card to the ceiling. The room is dark, but there is enough moonlight tonight that I can see the blurry outline of Simon's crooked heart overhead. I've got the new shoes Gran gave me tucked in by my bed. I have a lot to be grateful for. I won't think about Mom not showing up.

I don't know the time, but I hear my mom's car pull into the driveway. It doesn't make sense, but I want to run away. I don't want to face her. Don't want to cry. She creeps into the bedroom and gently tries to shake me awake. I keep my eyes shut, my body limp. Mom takes me up in her lap, stroking the hair off of my face, saying over and over, "I'm sorry, baby. I'm sorry."

When she finally leaves, I listen to her go downstairs. She talks for a few moments with Gran. Only a few words, I can't make them out, even though my ears are straining. Already a part of me is wishing that I'd let Mom know I had woken up. I would have been able to take in and enjoy the attention, all the

"I'm sorrys" and the hugs. But a larger part of me, the fist-hard part of me, the knot in my stomach, is glad that I didn't.

I hear the front door close and Mom's shoes cross the porch. I get out of bed and go to the window. I watch Mom's shadow figure go to her borrowed car, the inside of it lighting up as she opens the door and gets in. She sits down, shuts the door. She stays there a moment. Her hands on the steering wheel, not moving, her head bowed, and then the inside lights in the car fade out to blackness, and the front porch light flicks off.

I hear the creak of Gran's footsteps as she crosses the wood floor in the hall and goes to bed.

But still, I stay standing there. My body tucked back behind the window frame. It's all dark outside now. The car is just a silhouette. I listen to the night sounds. Crickets, frogs, trees shifting, an owl hoots once, twice, then is silent. Mom is still sitting there in her sealed-up car.

Then finally, I hear her start up the engine. Something about the noise of it, the car's engine turning over, agitates me. I want to run down the stairs, to my mom before it's too late. But it already is, because the car is backing up now, tires spitting gravel and dirt.

I make my body stay where it is, by the window. I watch as my mom's car turns around, then pulls out and heads down the long dirt driveway.

Nobody is standing on the porch, waving good-bye. Just the solitary beams of white-yellow light from the front of the car bouncing off the potholes and the beaten-up road, leading the way. The two red taillights follow, getting smaller and smaller until finally they blink out and she's gone.

● ● ● ●

When I get up this morning, Simon and Tessa are still pretty subdued. Watching me to make sure I'm okay. I don't know what to do. That's the problem when you fake things. You get caught in a bigger lie and a bigger one. Like me pretending to be asleep last night. Fine. It felt like a good solution at the time. But now, what about Simon and Tessa? I hadn't been thinking about them. They're walking around worried. They didn't sleep well thinking about Mom not showing.

But now, if I tell them she *did* show up. That once she remembered, she did make the effort. If I tell them that she borrowed her friend's car and drove all the way to Gran's from town, in the middle of the night, even though she had to work the next morning, then Simon and Tessa will wonder why I didn't wake them up. They might think I was being selfish. Mom came for a visit and I kept her all for myself. And I guess in a way it was selfish of me, when I think about it now. It just didn't feel like that at the time. I don't know why I pretended to be asleep. I should have woken up the kids when I heard her car pulling into our driveway. We could have run downstairs like it was Christmas morning and got the leftover cake out of the pantry. We could have had another birthday celebration in the middle of the night. It could have been special, fun, exciting. Something Simon and Tessa would have remembered the rest of their lives.

But no.

I pretended to be asleep. And now Simon and Tessa are looking over their shoulder, thinking, if Mom could forget about the birthday of her firstborn child, then neither of them is safe. She could just go away and forget about us and never come back.

I can't stop thinking about it, doing the morning chores, taking care of the chickens, the cow, over breakfast. There's no easy solution. Maybe I should talk it over with Gran? But then she'd know I'd faked it and pretended to be asleep when I wasn't. She might never trust me again. She might think I am an ungrateful sneak of a child who doesn't care about anyone but myself. Bad news, a hooligan, like those church ladies said. I can't tell Gran. There's no way out of this mess.

"See you," I say, grabbing my lunch, heading out the door for the bus. My bus gets here first. The elementary-school bus doesn't come for another half an hour.

"Bye." Tessa and Simon put little please-be-happy-Jack smiles on their faces. I feel sick.

Some skinny girl with acne plops herself down next to me

on the bus. She's got a cell phone glued to her ear. I don't know if Kate would have sat with me again or not. Anyway, when she gets on she sits with this pretty, dark-haired girl and they laugh and talk the whole way into town, and I try not to notice.

I didn't have time to do my social studies homework, with all the drama at home, and so the teacher says I have to come back at lunch and make it up. Oh, big deal! What a punishment! I'm not going to be able to go to the lunchroom and sit in a corner like a loser and eat lunch all by myself . . . Waaah.

I go through English class trying not to stress about it. Even though I won't miss the lunchroom, I've never been kept in before as a disciplinary action. I'm the one who gets mostly A's.

The lunch buzzer goes and I fight the flow of traffic back to my locker. I get my lunch sack and the binder with my social studies in it and make my way to Mr. Brames's classroom. I'm kind of nervous, my palms are a little sweaty, but I put on my who-cares face.

Mr. Brames is sitting behind his desk, with his face buried in a book, eating a tunafish sandwich. He barely looks up. "Take a seat," he says, and I do. I look around at the other kids. There's a couple of Goths, a couple of skaters, one big kid with broken glasses held together with tape, and me.

I take out my books and get to work. It's the fastest lunch hour I've had in a long time. I do yesterday's social studies homework and today's. My English assignment that isn't due until next Wednesday. Two pages of math. I even manage to eat most of my food before the lunch bell rings. Maybe I should try to get detention every day. It's an efficient use of time.

"All right," Mr. Brames says as the buzzer is sounding. "Off you go." Although really, saying that is just a formality, since the second the buzzer started blaring, half the detention group was already out the door.

● ● ● ●

Getting on the bus and everybody is pushing and shoving, scrambling for the best seats, and I hear a "Hey, Jack." At first I don't look up, figuring the person isn't calling me. There are a lot of Jacks in this school, and I don't know anybody.

I hear it again. "Jack! Hey, Jack." So I look up just in case, and it's a good thing I do, because there is that red-headed girl, Kate. She's got a prime seat in the back and she's smiling at me, saving me a space.

I return her wave and start pushing my way to where she is waiting. I sit myself down in this primo spot at the back of the bus where the cool kids hang and every pothole and bump in the road sends you soaring into the air.

"This is great!" I say. "You got great seats, Kate." She smiles proudly.

I'm about to say more, use my conversational skills, but this big, hairy-mammoth guy from eleventh or twelfth grade nudges my shoulder with his elbow and growls, "Hey, shrimp, that's my seat. Scram." Now if it was some other day, or I was sitting with someone else, maybe I would have got up from this seat and moved.

But it's today, and I didn't spend the last six months of my life teaching Simon how to deal with bullies for nothing.

"No," I say.

"Come on, brat!" he says, giving me a shove. "Get your ass in gear!"

The next thing I know, I've shot to my feet, my fists cocked, and I'm yelling at the top of my lungs, "Make me!" He looks kind of shocked, because this guy's really big. I come up to maybe his bellybutton. I know it's stupid. There is no way I can take this guy down. It doesn't matter how many fancy moves I know. I've got a cocky little grin on my face, like I'm not even scared. Because I am, but I'm angry too, like *No more! Enough!* All this weird energy pulses through me like a comic book superhero power.

"Come on!" I yell, fists up and ready, just like my dad taught me. "You want to fight?! I'll fight! But me and my friend aren't movin'!"

"Okay." He backs up a step or two, hands out, palms up. "Okay, take it easy . . . Jeez."

His friend standing behind him says, "Yeah. Let's forget it, Jake. She's just a girl . . ." They find somewhere else to sit while

I ease myself back down in my seat, my body hot and cold and then hot again. Everybody is twisted around in their seats, staring at me and at the big, lumbering Jake guy who is heading down the aisle. He sits in an empty seat at the front of the bus with the younger students. For a couple of seconds, it's quiet at the back, and then people start talking, a soft buzz at first and then louder. But I don't look around. I just hold my hands tight together in my lap, so no one can notice they're shaking. I don't want to look at Kate. I'm a little scared of what I'll see, scared she thinks I'm a nutcase. That she wishes she hadn't called me over to sit with her. I don't know why I went off like that. It was fine to do theses things in my old life. Everybody knew me. But here? And with a maybe new friend? What was I thinking?

I'm sitting here on this stupid bus, my face beet red. I can feel that everybody is still staring at me. Then I hear Kate say, "Wow . . ." almost under her breath. "That was Jake Glendale. You just stood up to Jake Glendale and lived to tell the story." She starts to laugh. "That was great, Jack! That was great!" She slaps me on the back, and a couple of other girls do too. Girls I didn't know, and a few boys too. I feel this relief rushing through me, that it was okay, people don't think I'm a crazy, out-of-control freak. I feel like I've dodged a bullet, a couple of them. And this big smile, which starts slow, spreads out over my whole entire face.

When I get home I tell the school-bus story to an admiring

audience of two. Gran thinks I was foolhardy and dumb. But Tessa and Simon make me tell the story over and over, laughing delightedly as I re-enact it. Leaping to my feet, fists cocked, looking way, way, up so that by the fourth time I've told the story, Jake Glendale's head is all the way up to the ceiling.

While we're eating, another problem is solved.

Gran says, "By the way, Jack, your mother came by last night, but you were asleep. She wanted me to tell you she loves you and she's sorry she missed your birthday."

"Oh. Okay." I say, looking down at my food, not quite able to meet Gran's eye. "Thanks for telling me, Gran. I'm glad Mom didn't miss my birthday." I sneak a look at Simon and Tessa and they're looking at Gran, like little birds, waiting for more crumbs. "See," I say. "Mom loves us. She didn't forget. Just got a little held up is all."

● ● ● ●

Things are going pretty well at school. It's nice having a friend again. I didn't realize how much I missed having someone to talk to.

I didn't know if there were going to be repercussions from the whole Jake Glendale thing, but apparently he didn't take offense. He thinks the whole thing was hilarious. Go figure. When he sees me in the halls, he says, "Hey, Spunky!" Sometimes he'll put up his big sledgehammer fists, but he'll do it like he's scared, his knees knocking together, a smile on his face. "Oh, man," he'll say. "Here she comes! Yikes!" Or sometimes he'll leap behind a friend half his size and hang on his arm, pretending to cower behind him, squeaking in a high girly voice, "Save me! Save me from Spunky!" Everybody laughs, because when Jake Glendale makes a joke, even if it's lame, you laugh. He's in twelfth grade and he's the biggest guy in the school by a long shot. He's even bigger than the teachers. So sometimes he pretends he's scared, and other times Big Jake will just ignore me, or nod, like we're buddies. "Spunky," he'll say and carry on talking with his friends.

So that whole bus incident was a very lucky thing. I'm not dead, and I'm sort of a mini-celebrity among the eighth-graders. I eat lunch with Kate now every day in the lunchroom, or sometimes, if it's nice, we'll take our lunch outside and eat on the field, stretch out, and get some sun.

Things are pretty good for me at school. Not so with Simon. It's harder for me to help him with his homework because I'm getting back from school much later than he and Tessa. I am also getting way more homework myself this year. I guess it's on account of having a different teacher for every subject. They all think they are the only one giving you homework, so they give a ton, all at the same time. It's a really dumb system. They should get together, give each subject a limit to how much they can load on you in one day. It's really not fair.

By the time I get back around quarter to five, Simon has already been struggling with his homework for more than an hour. I have to get changed into my home clothes and start my own homework. It's dinnertime. We eat. There's the cleanup to do, the chickens, the cow, lunches to make for tomorrow. Then I still have to finish my homework, but I also have to help Simon, because he's generally in tears by this time. No time to play, even though he's just a little kid in third grade. He should be outside, running around, playing catch, watching the sunset. But he doesn't want to get in trouble. He's really struggling, is behind the class. Way behind. Tonight, tucking Simon in, I can tell he's troubled.

"What are you thinking about, Simon?" I say.

"Hmm?" he looks up, slightly startled.

"What's on your mind?"

"Kyle," he says.

"What about Kyle?"

Simon doesn't answer.

"What about Kyle?" I repeat, keeping my voice, my face, pleasant and calm.

"He said . . . that . . ." Simon's face is working, trying not to cry, "That . . . I'll never have a wife."

"Why would he say something like that?"

"Because I'm stupid!" Simon says, suddenly impatient with me. Like I should be able to see what he's talking about without him having to spell it out. "And he says" – Simon is grouchy now – "that no girl would ever want to marry someone who's so stupid and can't even read."

"You can rea –" I start to say, but he cuts me off. All of a sudden Simon's yelling like a dam that's burst.

"I can't read! I *can't* read! You *know* that!" Kicking off his covers, throwing his worn-out, sad-faced, stuffed donkey to the floor.

"Yes, you can –"

"No! I can't! I *can't!*" He storms over to the bookshelf and starts pulling books out, throwing them to the floor. "I can't read *that!* I can't read *that!* Or *that!*" I have to grab a hold of him and pin his arms to his sides before he destroys our room. Tessa comes out of the bathroom in her pajamas, toothbrush in hand, mouth full of foam.

"You can read, Simon," I say. "You can. It just takes you a while, is all . . ."

"No, I can't, *I can't* . . ." He's sobbing now, curling up small in a ball in my arms like somebody is kicking him in the stomach. "I can't *tell* what the words are." He turns his anguished tear-stained face up to mine. "I can't read the street signs. I can't read the words the teacher prints on the board. How am I ever going to grow up? Kyle's right. Nobody's ever going to . . . want to . . . marry such a dummy . . . What am I going to do? How am I going to get a job? Take care of myself? I'm scared, Jack. I'm scared."

I don't know what to do. What can I say? I can't lie anymore. He can't read. I don't know if he'll ever be able to.

I pat him on the back. Soothe him with my hands. "There, there," I say, but it's not enough. Not even a smidgen of comfort. "I'm here," I say. "Jack's here . . . Tessa too."

"Yeah," says Tessa. "I'm here." She wraps her arms around Simon too. She accidentally swipes me with her slobbery toothbrush, but I don't yell at her. This is more important. And we stay like that, me kneeling, Tessa standing, our arms, our bodies, like a shield, encasing Simon. Tom pushes his wet nose between me and Tessa and manages to get at Simon's tear-stained face. He plants big, wet dog kisses all over Simon's face, his nose, his eyes, his cheeks, his chin. Then when Tom's covered every inch of Simon's face, he moves to Simon's neck, and Simon starts giggling, even though he's sad, because Simon's got a ticklish neck. Tessa and I start smiling and laughing too, because we're relieved, and Simon laughs a sort of tumbly laugh, like clear creek water, jumping and dancing over round, smoothed-out rocks, that makes you feel like everything's right and good in the world.

After we straighten up the books and put them back on the shelf, we remake Simon's bed. Tessa tucks his stuffed donkey back in its place of honor, overseeing the room. Then we go downstairs, even though it's after Simon and Tessa's bedtime. Even though they've brushed their teeth. We sneak into the pantry, bare feet and tiptoes, and I get down my leftover birthday cake where I was storing it on the top shelf. We sit cross-legged on the cold pantry floor and we polish that baby off. Then, for a special treat, I let them get into bed again without rebrushing their teeth.

● ● ● ●

I'm having a bad day. The cow ran away. I missed my bus. Gran wouldn't give me a ride. She made me walk, and thanks to her my feet were like raw hamburger by the time I got to school. Those birthday shoes Gran bought me may be pretty, but they sure are tough on the feet. I have blisters all over, on both heels and on five of my toes. The worst part was that once I got there, I couldn't take the stupid shoes off. You aren't allowed to walk around barefoot.

I missed the first two periods. I arrived partway through the third. I had to sign in late at the office.

It was really pointless to make me walk all the way to school. For what? A scrap of third period, lunch, Phys. Ed., French, and Art.

Now I hop back on the bus and head home. My feet are throbbing like an elephant has been Riverdancing on them.

When I get off the bus, I wait until it disappears round the bend. I don't even pretend to walk, just flop my tired body down there beside the ditch. Once the bus is gone, I rip those shoes off, my socks too, and walk home barefoot. Painful? Anything is better than wearing those shoes.

I limp in through the back door, and what greets me at the kitchen table? A note from Simon's new teacher, Mrs. Lederer. She's "requesting" a meeting with Simon's parents/guardians at two o'clock Wednesday. That's the day after tomorrow. It's parent/teacher conferences and usually it's optional, but this time it's not. She has already written in an appointment time and highlighted it with a yellow marker. So there is no mistaking her intention. Not to mention the handwritten note on the side of the regular photocopied form: *Please make sure to come. Thanks. – Mrs. Lederer*, with a fake friendly smiley face drawn in pencil.

I'm reading this note, and it's like my belly has just dropped down through the kitchen floor, because I know what all this friendliness means. She doesn't want Simon in her class. She wants to fail him. She thinks he's stupid, "lazy," and it's not fair! She doesn't even know him! She hasn't even given him a chance!

"What is it?" Simon asks, looking up at me.

"Oh, nothing much," I say, but my face feels stiff, like a mask. If Simon is looking closely he'll know something's wrong.

"Am I . . . in trouble?"

"No, honey," I say. "It's just parent/teacher conferences. Everybody has them."

"Is Mom going?"

"You know Mom can't go. It's a workday. She can't get off work."

"Well who's going? Gran?"

"No. We don't want Gran to know about this, remember? Don't tell Gran."

"Who's going to come? Mrs. Lederer said someone's got to come. She was very clear about that. She said it was important."

"I'll come," I say. "I'll come see your teacher."

"She said my mom or my dad."

"Our mom can't come and our dad's dead, so I'm the next best thing. Don't worry, kid. It'll be fine. You'll see." But I don't know yet what I'm going to do. How I'm going to get out of school?

I'll come up with something. "Don't worry, little dude," I say. And I go upstairs to soak my sore feet.

● ● ● ●

I didn't sleep well last night. I noticed dark smudges under my eyes this morning as I was washing my face with cold water and soap and pulling my hair back in one of Gran's hair clips so I'll look older, more mature.

I went to bed early enough. That wasn't the problem. It was my thoughts and worries. They were like seagulls crowding around the back of a fishing boat. Diving, swooping, squabbling over fish guts. The minute I made my brain let go of one fear, it seized onto the tail of another. I went over my plan again and again. How to exit my school grounds without getting caught. Skipping out, essentially. Some people might call it playing hooky, but I don't. To me, if I was ever to *play* hooky, it would be something carefree, fun, that I'd do with friends. This feels anything but.

I leave school at lunchtime. I carry everything with me to my last class, so when the buzzer sounds, I'm able just to get up and go.

I act like I'm just walking to the end of the soccer field, then I take a quick glance around to make sure there are no teachers looking. The coast is clear. I slip through a gap in the fence and scramble down the slope to the bushes. I'm careful not to slide on my butt. I don't want to get my skirt dirty. I follow the road from a distance, staying under cover behind bushes and trees until the school is well out of sight.

I dressed carefully this morning. Last night, I pressed my khaki skirt and blue-and-white tuck-in shirt with Gran's ancient iron. It doesn't even have a steamer. I have to have a cupful of water at hand, dip my fingers in, and then sprinkle the drops of water on the clothes before I put the hot iron on them.

"Why are you putting your clothes out on the chair like that?" Simon asked me last night, sitting cross-legged on his bed, wearing his Spider-Man pajamas that are getting too short. I can almost see skin at the elbows, the knees, and in the behind section of his pajamas that are especially threadbare.

"Getting ready," I said. "Just getting ready, big guy."

"Why?"

"I want to look nice to meet your teacher," I said. That's all I said. I didn't say anything about my fears and what I think the topic of conversation is going to be. No sense in scaring him. "Now, don't forget, you guys," I said to Tessa and Simon. "What do you do tomorrow?"

Tessa looked up from her book. "We pretend we're going to school, and then once we're down the road we double-back through the bushes to the barn."

"And where do you go in the barn?"

"The hayloft."

"And what do you do there?"

"We hide," Tessa had said. She was looking a little nervous.

"And don't make any noise so Gran won't know we're there, and eat the special treats you left for us in the grain bin!" Simon had said happily, like everything was going to work out okay and this was a fun, exciting adventure.

I'm out of view of school now, but still I'm half walk-running, Dad's wristwatch bouncing gently against my chest. It's a comforting feeling. Like he's with me on this.

Last night, lying in bed, thinking about what I was going to have to do. I couldn't sleep. Me trying to pass myself off to Simon's teacher is more than a little scary. I waited until Tessa turned out the light. Then I got Dad's watch out from under my pajama top and brought it up to my cheek, the *tick, tick* sound very faint through my closed-up hand and all the tape holding it together. The ticking noise was almost inaudible. I do this sometimes when I'm real scared. I pretend it's my dad's hand holding the watch. That it's his knuckles brushing my cheek, not mine. I pretend that he's here with me, guiding me and making me strong.

I'm not sure how long it's going to take me to walk to Simon's school. I got directions off the Web in the computer lab yesterday at lunch. But that was driving directions. I have no idea how long walking will take. I've had to guess and have left myself lots of time to spare. I would rather be early than late.

I'm wearing my running shoes and I have my good shoes stuffed into my backpack along with all my homework and my lunch, because even though I know runners clash with this outfit, I learned my lesson the other day. My poor feet come before my vanity. They're still recuperating, all covered in bandages. I'll put my good shoes on when I arrive at Simon's school.

I walk fast for two reasons. One, I don't want the truant officer to pick me up, if there is one. It's kind of like werewolves, people always talk about truant officers, but I don't know anybody who has actually met one. Or has first-hand knowledge of them. I've never seen proof that truant officers really exist.

The second reason I walk fast is because, although I left plenty of time, the minute I slipped out past the gate and got down the slope, hidden from view, once I had the leaving-my-school-without-permission fear over with, the I-hope-I-don't-get-lost-and-these-directions-are-correct worry took over. So I walk extra fast so that if I do get lost, I'll still have time to figure out where I went wrong and find my way back again.

I get to Simon and Tessa's school in good time. One thirty-two by Dad's watch. And Dad's watch is accurate. He was always on time. I have almost half an hour to spare. Simon's classroom is room eight.

I don't go to his class directly. I sit out back of the school, on the side of a cement planter with a scrawny tree stuffed in it that looks half-dead. Probably needs water.

I change into my good shoes, try to eat some of my lunch, but I don't have much appetite. Stomach in knots. Arguments, persuasions forming, playing over and over in my head. Things Simon's teacher might say, how I can combat, counter them.

Change her mind. Mrs. Lederer. Her name is Mrs. Lederer. I'm not familiar with her from last spring.

One thirty-eight. Time's crawling.

I put away my lunch. Smooth down my hair again with my hands, reattach Gran's clip. Stand up. Sit down. Take out my lunch. Look through it again, like maybe something new has appeared in there. It hasn't. I return it to my backpack. One forty-two.

I wonder what his teacher's going to say. I mean, I know what she's going to say, nothing good. But I wonder *how* she is going to say it. I wonder what Mrs. Lederer's like? Nobody else has forced a parent/teacher conference on us. So that's one thing I already know, that she's pushy and I don't like her.

My shoes are killing my feet, even with these bandages.

One forty-five. I guess I'll start walking over to the classroom, that'll take a few minutes. Then I'll be there, ready.

One forty-eight. It took three minutes to walk here from the back. The door of the classroom is shut, but through its window I can see a mother and a father sitting perched in little kid chairs, like oversized storks. They are facing someone behind a desk. I crick my neck a bit, but it doesn't help because of the way the sunlight is hitting the window. I can't see what the person behind the desk looks like, just the parents. The mom is laughing now and the dad is smiling. They look proud, like all the news they're getting today is good. I don't know why this makes me feel sad. It's a happy thing that some lucky kid's got a mom and dad and a picture-perfect life.

One fifty-one. Nine minutes to go. Nine more minutes. I wipe my palms off on the back of my skirt and sit down on the metal bench. It has faded blue paint flecking off of it and a bit of rust around the bolts. I smooth my skirt out flat, trying to slow down my heart. I take deep breaths. I cross my legs. I place my hands in my lap, folded and composed, like maybe a parent would do. I want to look at my dad's watch again. I really feel the need to hold it on my cheek, but I don't. If I can see in, then the people in the classroom can see out, and I don't want to do anything to look foolish. I've got to do a good job here. Simon's counting on it.

The door opens, the mom and dad come out. They're still smiling. She's pregnant.

"Thanks again," the mom says.

"My pleasure. Your daughter is a joy," the woman holding the doorknob says. Then her head comes into view as they shake hands. It's Mrs. Lederer. It has to be.

Mrs. Lederer doesn't go back inside right away, so I get a good look at her. She isn't at all what I expected. She has short, steel-gray hair, cut in a bob, but not a harsh one. She has soft, sort of tumbly curls. Bold red earrings that match the lipstick she is wearing. Glasses. Modern stylish ones, like the ones they show on the TV commercials. She glances around, her eyes sliding past me on the bench, up the walkway. Then she looks the other way, toward the cement sidewalk that leads up to the parking lot, her earrings swinging. She waits for a moment. I would talk to her and introduce myself, but she seems like she's deep in thought. She lifts her shoulders and rotates them a bit, like they're stiff. Looks down past me again. Her eyes narrowing slightly, then she goes back inside, leaving the door propped open.

I take my dad's watch out and look at the time. One fifty-eight. Two minutes to go. A fat blackfly buzzes, lands on my shin, tries to taste the salt on my skin, but I don't let it. I shoo it away with my foot. One fifty-nine. One minute to go. I don't know if I should go in, or wait out here until she comes and gets me. The fly lands again. On my forearm this time. I shake it off. Two o'clock. It's two o'clock now. Do I go in? Or do I wait out here? It's fifteen seconds after two. I'm late now, and there's no one inside with her, so I think I'd better go in.

I stand up. My mouth is dry. I wish I had some water. I think briefly about running down to the water fountain at the end of this row of classrooms, but it's now two o'clock and the second hand is marching around the face of Dad's watch pretty fast. I go up to the door and knock, even though it's open. I figure it's probably more polite that way.

Mrs. Lederer looks up from her stack of paperwork she has in front of her on the desk.

"Yes?" she says. "Can I help you?" Like she thinks I'm lost or something.

"Yes," I say. "I'm here for my brother."

"Oh, I'm sorry, we didn't have school today. It's parent/ teacher conferences, maybe he's at a –"

"That's what I'm here for, ma'am." I say, sounding way more confident than I feel. I take a step into the room, so she'll know I'm in the right place. "The conference. You're Mrs. Lederer, right?"

"Yes, but . . ." The two train-track lines between her eyebrows, rising up out of the nosepiece of her glasses, deepen.

"I'm Jacqueline Miriam Cooper. Simon Cooper's sister. I'm here to represent Simon's family for the conference." I smile and stick out my hand for shaking so we can get it over with and she'll let me sit down in one of those miniature chairs and get started. I don't want her to start nitpicking about the "parent" part of this equation.

The strategy doesn't work. She doesn't shake my hand.

"Shouldn't you be in school, dear?" she says.

"I took the afternoon off to come to the conference. I'm here for the conference." I'm trying to keep my voice calm, but I'm getting a bad feeling in my belly. A panicky this-isn't-going-to-go-well feeling.

"I'm sorry, dear," she says, shaking her head.

"No." I say, cutting her off. "I'm here for the conference. The Simon Cooper conference."

"I appreciate you making the effort to come down, but you simply won't do. I need to speak to your father or mother."

"They can't come."

"Why?"

"They just can't!" Why's she being so dumb?

"Why?"

"It's *none* of your business, okay?" And I'm trying not to lose my temper, but it's really hard. I can hear my voice getting more and more shrill.

"I beg to differ. It is my business. All of my students are my business. Especially a student who is struggling as much as your brother is. Now I want you to go home and tell your mother and/or father that it is imperative that I speak with them. Do you understand me?"

"Listen, lady. They aren't coming. I don't know why you can't get that into your skull. They're never coming. So all you got is me."

"If they won't come to me," she says, acting oh-so-calm-and-reasonable, "I'll come to them."

"Forget it!" I yell. "Just forget it! God, you're stupid." I storm out the door, slamming it hard. I don't even care that the mom waiting on the bench gives me a dirty look. I don't even care. It's just more mean gossip this stupid town can chew on. "She was screaming at poor Mrs. Lederer, can you imagine the nerve?"

It's a long walk home under the best circumstances, but with the failure of my parent/teacher conference, my body feels like I'm pushing myself uphill in a snowstorm. Everything heavy and an effort.

It takes a very long time to get home. And what's the first thing I see when I walk into the living room?

Gran is sitting in her rocking chair, sucking on her teeth, reading over one of those Serenity Valley flyers. "Oh my," she's saying under her breath. "Oh my, doesn't this look fine."

I'm going to strangle Tessa and Simon! I told them over and over: "I'm going to be coming home late tomorrow. So, when it's time for you to sneak back out to the road and pretend to come home from school, make sure you check the mailbox while you're out there. Okay? If there are any Serenity Valley flyers, bury them in the garbage. Okay? Don't forget. It's very important."

"Okay," they said. "Okay, Jack, we'll check. You can count on us." Apparently not!

I stand there, stuck in the doorway. "What are you reading, Gran?" I say, even though any idiot with half a brain can see perfectly well what it is.

"Oh, Jack. You're home," she says, looking up with a smile. "I'm looking at this Serenity Valley flyer. The place looks nice.

I can see why Mabel is so fond of it. Weekly maid service. My, my. That certainly is the high life."

I walk over, my mouth dry as cotton. I make myself look over Gran's shoulder at the Serenity Valley flyer like I've never seen it before. "I don't know . . ." I start to say, but there's a knock on the front door. An authoritative knock that means business.

"Who could that be?" Gran asks.

"I have no idea," I say, but I know it can't be good. Good news doesn't drop in unexpected. Good news doesn't knock like that.

When Gran and I get into the hall, I can see through the window who it is standing on our porch. It's Simon's teacher, Mrs. Lederer. I don't know how she found out where we live. Needless to say, my heart is not jumping for joy.

"Who's that?" Gran says. And for one brief moment I'm hoping that she decides to turn around and walk away, but she doesn't. She shuffles over to the door, looking older and more disheveled than usual, opens it. "What do you want?" Gran says, no social chitchat for her.

"Hello," Mrs. Lederer says, cool as can be. Like she's not standing on our front porch uninvited. "You must be Doris Findlay, Simon's grandmother."

"Great-grandmother," says Gran, looking at her suspiciously over the top of her bifocals. "Do I know you?"

"I'm Mrs. Lederer, Simon's teacher. I'm sorry to barge in on you like this. However, after my little conversation with Jacqueline this afternoon, I felt the need to dig a bit farther. I pulled his file at the office. I feel it is vital that I have a face-to-face conversation with whoever is Simon's legal guardian."

"Is he in trouble?" Gran says. She sounds worried, like she cares.

"No . . . Well, actually, yes." Mrs. Lederer is feeling her way around the words. "But not in the way that you mean. He's a good boy. He tries hard. It's that he's having difficulty learning."

"You better come in and sit down," Gran says, holding the door open.

"Thank you. That would be lovely. Hello, Jacqueline," Mrs. Lederer says, nodding at me. I nod back as polite as I can, my face a mask. I'm in deep shit now.

I follow them into the living room. There's no way I'm going to leave the two of them alone together. We all sit. Gran in her rocker, Mrs. Lederer and me on the sofa. I try to look all relaxed and comfortable, like I wasn't just screaming at this woman this afternoon like a crazed banshee.

"This is the thing," Mrs. Lederer jumps right in. "I believe that Simon has a learning disability. I'm not a specialist, but I have been teaching elementary school children for thirty-four years and one learns to recognize the signs pretty quickly. I feel that he should be tested, and would benefit greatly by being involved in our special needs program."

"Needs? You want to put Simon in special needs?" I say, shooting off the sofa, so much for being cool and relaxed. "I don't think so!"

"Jack," Gran says, sounding none too pleased. "Sit down. Let the woman speak."

But I can't sit down. I can't just sit here all nicey-nice and let them put Simon in with the needs kids. No way. "You don't understand, Gran. You haven't seen those kids in needs. You haven't! I mean, I don't have anything against them, but God, some of them are really weird!"

"Jack! I mean it. Sit down and hold your tongue, or get out."

I sit down. Mrs. Lederer starts talking again. Blah . . . blah . . . blah . . . I watch her mouth moving up and down, but nothing much is going in. I hear a word every now and then, that's about it. "Electrical impulses . . . blah . . . blah . . . blah . . . " "The brain. . . blah. . . blah. . . blah. . . " "Dyslexia . . . blah . . . blah . . . possibly dysgraphia . . ." Whatever the hell that means. She's making poor Simon sound like a friggin' science project. I wait for her to run out of gas and for Gran to finish up with her questions. I don't say a word. I just sit on that sofa, my mouth glued shut, and send Mrs. Lederer hate waves with my eyes. I bet she can feel them too, because she won't even look in my direction.

Finally she leaves and good riddance. "Gran," I say the minute the door closes behind her. "You can't sign those papers. I'm serious. You have no idea how bad the other kids rag on the special needs kids."

"It sounds to me," Gran says, "that Simon has a real problem and this might help him. You know, my Horace had difficulty with this kind of thing, but we never had a name for it."

"Gran! Did you *hear* what I said?" And I'm trying not to yell, I'm trying not to get all emotional, but I've worked too hard with Simon to let them just throw away any chance he has of fitting in. "You just *can't*!"

"Stop crying, girl. Let's talk about this sensibly. Apparently Simon can't read or write."

"He can read a bit and write too," I insist. "He can. It's just that he's a little slow. A lot of boys are. He'll catch up. I promise."

"Would you stop your bawling. There is no need for this kind of emotional display," Gran snaps. "I'm not an ogre. Let's be reasonable about this. What Simon's teacher is recommending –"

"I'll work with him harder. I will. You *can't* put him in special needs, Gran. He gets bullied bad enough as it is, but this would be social suicide! That's why I've been teaching him how to punch and stuff, because things suck for him at school. They really suck!"

"I want to try," a small voice says. My head whips around. Gran's does too.

"What?" I say, even though I heard Simon clearly the first time. There he is, sitting on the stairs. I didn't even see him there. Tessa neither. Both of them, hunched down, side by side, like they've been sitting there listening for a very long time. Don't know why I'm so shocked. I've listened in on many conversations myself in that very same spot.

"I said, I want to go," Simon says, his voice wavering a bit. "I want to learn how to read and write. I want to be like the rest of the kids. And if going to special needs will help me with that, I want to go."

"But . . . " I say, feeling a little lost. "Simon, kids are going to tease you."

"So what?" he stands up, juts his chin out a bit. "They already do." He shoves his hands in his pockets. "Anyway, enough of this yakking. I'm starving. What's for dinner?"

And that's that. End of the conversation. He and Tessa come down the stairs, her arm still around his shoulders, and off they go into the kitchen. Gran follows. No one left here in the hall to argue with. I make a pit stop in the bathroom to give my nose a blow, splash cold water on my face. Feel like the whole world's turned upside down.

Throughout dinner and the cleanup, nobody talked about it. It's like the whole Mrs. Lederer conversation never happened.

Tessa brought up Serenity Valley. Which with Simon's special needs crisis, I'd totally forgot about. At first I was mad that she reminded Gran, but apparently Gran thought those worries we had were a joke. "I have no desire whatsoever to park my bony butt up at that glorified old age home. No, they are going to have to carry me out of this house in my coffin, because that's the only way I'm going to leave this place." Not only that but she said as long as she's breathing, we're welcome to stay.

It was an odd feeling for me at dinner. All this chatter going on around me, everyone moving on, making plans, and I was just sitting there. It's like everything, every tiny little particle of my body had been clenched tight for such a long time that it got tired out. All at once, gave up, and poof, the tension was gone. Drained out of me and I was sitting there, empty.

I spend Saturday in a fog, doing my chores mechanically. Milk the cow, feed the chickens. Muck out the barn. At dinner, it's just me, Gran, and Simon, as Tessa has gone on a sleepover. Still wiped out, I tuck Simon in and go to bed early. When I wake up Sunday morning, the worries are back. Not the Gran and Serenity Valley and no-place-to-live ones. Those ones are gone. But the Simon worries are eating at me big-time. I don't know if I should bring it up, though. Because if Simon's going to special needs, I don't want to make it worse for him by making him carry my concerns as well as his own.

Church, as always, is boring. But generally it's worth it, because Sunday-night dinner is always good. Gran pulls out all the stops for Sunday dinner, and I saw a fresh apple pie cooling on the kitchen counter earlier, filling the kitchen with its delicious aroma. Cinnamon, sweet fall apples, baked into bubbling juicy goodness, a dash of nutmeg. Gran's pies are the best, bar none.

By the time we get back, the smell of the pie has spread throughout the rest of the house. I can even smell it up here in the upstairs bathroom where I am changing out of my church-going clothes back into my home ones. I'm thinking maybe I'll go for a swing. Sort things out a bit in my mind. There's something about swinging that does that sometimes. As I'm coming out of the bathroom, I see Simon walking into the bedroom. He's deep in thought. I think he must be worrying too. He's probably rethinking the needs situation just like me.

"Hey, little dude," I say. "What's on your mind?" Because maybe he wants to talk.

He looks up, startled, caught. "What?" he says.

"What were you thinking about?"

He hesitates.

"You don't have to tell me if you don't want," I say. "You're entitled to your own thoughts." Because he is.

"I'll tell you," he says slowly, "but you have to promise" – a slow secret smile spreading out across his face – "not to tell anybody."

I'm relieved, because it's obvious this is not about school.

"I promise," I say. "I won't tell anyone. On all that is sacred and holy. This will be our secret, forever and ever."

"Until death do us part," Simon says, holding his palm upward, facing me.

"Until death do us part," I say solemnly, even though it's kind of a goofy thing to say. It's supposed to be part of the wedding vows, but I guess Simon doesn't know that. I place my palm against his and the pact is set.

"All right!" Simon says. "We've got to lock Tom in. He can't come. He'd ruin it." We lock Tom in the closet, because if we left him in the bathroom or the bedroom, Tessa might let him out when she comes home.

"Okay," Simon says, slapping his hands together like there's dust on his palms, or flour. "Let's go."

We go down the stairs together and out the back door. Simon's little body is practically vibrating with muffled excitement. I'm curious. Really curious. I'm starting to feel quite excited myself.

"Now, when we get there, you can't make noise," he whispers as we cross the back field. "You have to be quiet. Very, very quiet. Promise, okay?"

"Okay, I promise," I whisper. "Where are we going?"

His chest puffs up with importance. "You'll see . . . You'll see," he says, hand sneaking up, trying to cover the huge smile that has spread across his entire face. "We're almost there."

And I'm filled with happiness, crossing that field. Because if Simon can feel this way, if he can be dancing such a happy, gangly jig, as we beat our way through the waist-high grass, going toward what? His surprise. His secret. That his face can glow like this, be so full of magic, knowing that tomorrow Gran's handing in the permission papers and he's going to be put into a special needs class. Maybe everything's going to be okay. Maybe.

"I love you, Simon!" I give him a fierce hug, even though he doesn't want one and squirms free.

"Stop it!" he growls. "I'm not a baby!" His brow furrowed. "We have to be quiet. I'm in charge."

"Sorry . . . I forgot," I say, acting properly chastised, but my heart is soaring. "Let's go. I won't do it again."

"Okay," Simon says, a quick nod. "Let's go."

"All right," I whisper.

We get to the end of the back field and climb over the weathered wood fence. We're in the old abandoned apple orchard now. Nobody comes down here. The apples have gone wild and are too small to bother picking. Most of them are no bigger than a walnut or a plum.

"Shhh . . ." Simon puts his finger up against his lips. "Shhhh . . ." no louder than the whisper of the wind in the trees. We are both silent now, picking up and placing our feet carefully. I don't know why we are being so quiet, but I do it anyway. I can hear the rush and catch of my breath.

Simon stops abruptly and gestures me to do the same. We stand, our arms dangling, our eyes, supersensitive, looking everywhere all at once.

I don't see or hear anything.

"Pick up apples," he mouths, and then he squats down and starts gathering apples. He's staying down low, walking an odd sort of crab walk on his haunches, collecting the apples in his tucked-up shirt that he has made an apron out of and is holding the bottom end of in his teeth. When he's collected a batch, he methodically puts them down, all in the same spot, making a mound of apples on the ground. I gather apples too.

We make a huge pile of these Ping-Pong ball–sized apples, and then, when we have enough, Simon gestures that we sit down and wait. And we do. We wait in that orchard, in the late-morning mist that hasn't quite burnt off. I breathe in deep. The air is turning crisp, full of the smell of autumn and apples. It's a beautiful morning, the leaves just starting to change, a tinge of color on the outside edges.

We wait for a long time. And then I feel it. I feel it before

I see it. Simon's body tenses, giving it away. A rustle in the bushes.

"Don't move," Simon whispers. An animal of some kind sticks its nose first, and then its head, out from the underbrush. I'm not sure what it is yet. It's not big. It sniffs, then there is more rustling, and an old porcupine waddles out of the brush. A porcupine!

"Simon!" I whisper. Porcupines mean trouble. "Simon!" But he just gestures for me to keep quiet. He doesn't even look at me, his lit-up face and eyes are only on the porcupine. And I want to grab him up in my arms and run screaming, but I don't. Something about the expression on his face stops me, even though I am shaking all over. I stay and try not to think about old Tom and the damage these porcupines do to him.

The porcupine hesitates when it sees me. It looks at me long and hard with its black button eyes. "Come on," Simon whispers. "Come on." And it's like the porcupine makes a decision. It decides to trust me. It comes over to us, to Simon, who is squatted down, holding out an apple in his upturned palm. The porcupine scuttles forward a little, backs up, eyes on me, trying to determine if I'm going to pounce. Edges forward again, little by little, until it snatches the apple out of Simon's outstretched hand, backs up a few steps, to be out of grabbing range, and sits up on its hind legs, which I didn't know porcupines do. Then, with the apple firmly clutched in its front paws, the porcupine starts to eat. Nibble . . . nibble . . . nibble . . . Rotating the apple, just like a human. When the porcupine finishes the apple, it tosses the core over its shoulder and waddles forward again.

"You give him one," Simon says in a low, calm voice. So I hold out an apple from the pile, cautious, careful.

The porcupine looks at Simon, looks at me, and then edges forward, snatches the apple out of my palm, backs up and starts eating.

I don't know how many apples we feed that porcupine, but a lot, eighteen or twenty. I don't know how its stomach holds all of them. And I think that it's over, but Simon whispers, "Watch now." And I do. I watch as the porcupine shakes itself, hard, like a dog that's just got out of the water. It gives itself a good shaking and then . . . the porcupine lays down its quills. Flattens them down like a cardhouse flicked with your thumb. Then that porcupine waddles over to us, one last time, and Simon whispers to me, his face like a saint, "Pet it. We can pet it now." He reaches out, and I do too, and we pet that porcupine. We pet it and we pet it. And it is the softest thing I have ever felt in my whole life. Softer than Gran's gosling-down powderpuff that she got from her mom. Because underneath all those sharp, dangerous quills, the porcupine has this downy, delicate hair. It's the most amazing thing that I have ever experienced in my entire life.

When the porcupine has had enough, it steps away and shakes itself out. All its quills springing up and sticking out, razor sharp, and it looks like a porcupine again, all bristly and fierce.

"Wow," I whisper.

"Yeah," Simon breathes. And the porcupine turns itself around and, without a backward glance, walks back to the edge of the woods and disappears again, into the brush.

● ● ● ●

ACKNOWLEDGEMENTS

I would like to thank Kathy Lowinger for seeing a YA writer lurking in me that I didn't know I was, and for all of her editing suggestions and ideas. My thanks also go to Heather Sangster for her careful, meticulous polishing and fine-tuning. Both of you have truly made this book shine. I'd like to thank Terri Nimmo for the beautiful interior design and the inspired cover and Sean Tai for his scrupulous typesetting. Pam Osti and Kate Newman, thank you for getting the word out.

I'd like to thank my husband, Don, Ken Freeman, John Calley, and Diana Napper for being my friends, my comfort, my cheerleaders. You patiently read all my manuscripts before anyone else. I appreciate your helpful critiques and editing suggestions. My thanks also to my agent, Charlotte Sheedy, and to Meredith Kaffel, her assistant extraordinaire.

And last but not least, my thanks to all the people in distribution, the book reps and buyers, the bookstore owners and librarians. These are the people who are responsible for getting my book into the hands of the reading public. A most important job, and I am very grateful.